adrienne

maree brown

MAROONS

D1524049

BLACK DAWN Ⓐ SERIES

With the Black Dawn series we honor anarchist traditions and follow the great Octavia E. Butler's legacy, Black Dawn seeks to explore themes that do not reinforce dependency on oppressive forces (the state, police, capitalism, elected officials) and will generally express the values of antiracism, feminism, anticolonialism, and anticapitalism. With its natural creation of alternate universes and world-building, speculative fiction acts as a perfect tool for imagining how to bring forth a just and free world. The stories published here center queerness, Blackness, antifascism, and celebrate voices previously disenfranchised, all who are essential in establishing a society in which no one is oppressed or exploited. Welcome, friends, to Black Dawn!

BLACK DAWN SERIES #3

SANINA L. CLARK, SERIES EDITOR

Copyright 2023 by adrienne maree brown
This edition copyright 2023, AK Press (Chico / Edinburgh)
ISBN 9781849354806
E-ISBN 9781849354813
LCCN: 2022935890

AK Press   AK Press
370 Ryan Ave. #100   33 Tower Street
Chico, CA 95973   Edinburgh, Scotland EH6 7BN
www.akpress.org   akuk.com

Cover art by Juan Carlos Barquet, www.jcbarquet.com
Cover design and logo by T. L. Simons, tlsimons.com
Printed in the USA

"We must transform ourselves to transform the world."
—*Grace Lee Boggs*

MAROONS

Section I

The Dream of Every Cell is to Become Two

chapter one

Night

In the new moon dark, a small child slipped, alone, through the iron gates of the Warren community garden. It was cold enough for snow, but the air was dry. The child wore an adult's sweater that hung down to his ankles, over toddler leggings that were shorter each day. His head was wrapped in a scarf.

He moved stealthily between the deflated, wildish rows of leafy shadows, looking for anything familiar. He finally started pulling at everything he could touch until he found shapes he recognized—long pointy carrots, rock-hard beets, fat dense cabbage, bulbs of garlic and onions, and something else plentiful that might be green beans or peas.

He rolled up the bottom of his sweater, creating a pocket in front of him. Storing his small harvest like a baby kangaroo, he crept to the edge of the garden and slipped back out to the street. He looked left, toward home, and the way was clear. To his right, beyond a muted streetlight, there was something.

It was too black at first to see it, but the dark in the darkness moved closer to him. The child got very still down to his cells, the way he knew to disappear in plain sight. The darkness got still too—but there was breath visible in the air. Finally the darkness stepped into the pale beam cast by the streetlight.

The shadows relinquished a dog who looked like it was smiling at him, medium sized, furry, tail wagging slowly. This was unusual—since humans became scarce, creatures usually ran from Jizo. Sometimes they looked at him with hunter eyes and he had to spread his adult sweater arms wide to make of himself a menace.

But faced with this friendly creature, the child smiled back, opening the hand that wasn't holding his sweater, letting the dog come to him. The dog sniffed the boy's outstretched palm, then his neck, arm pits, crotch, down to his feet. The boy stifled a giggle. He took a few steps toward home and looked back. The dog was right behind him and caught up quickly. The boy was grateful for the friend to walk him home.

. . . .

She was standing outside the house, in a body that wasn't her own.

In front of her, up on the porch, was someone she loved, she knew him. He was trying to open the door, but he kept missing it. He turned around to face her, looking past her.

"What's wrong? You dead or something?" She called out, but he didn't respond. His eyes didn't even shadow like they normally did when he'd ignore her. He stomped down the porch stairs and went around the side of the house. She wants to follow him, but her body moves slowly. She wants to follow him, but she is stuck.

chapter two

The Radio

"Welcome, welcome one and all—and I mean every single one of y'all—to the Everything Awesome Circus, yes absolutely named after the best movie of all time, *The Lego Movie*! It's. So. Fucking. Wonderful to be here with you, each one of you, again, here in this small and seemingly empty but possibly, and probably, abundant place, this palace, this palatial place I still and now call home. If you can hear me that means nearly nothing at all about you, you fucking feds ... but you? Yes, you! If *you* can comprehend, I mean truly integrate this wisdom and magic pouring through me, this cosmic-conduiting-then/no-farce-now, no shitting, there is no end to how amazing this day can be. This only-day-we-have, this only-moment that has no end except the constant end in that funky blend of reflection we call moonlight that comes every night—and these days with no man-made competition it's so bright it's nearly a fright. A beautiful fucking fright! Except on these silent killer new moon nights where there's not a solar reflection in sight—now there are no babies here, but you and me? We know the worst things don't just come out at night and I will tell you why, no lie: it's a fucking nightmare out there! Be one with the suffering of this real world my friends. You have to see the grim shadow level of the inferno we face out there, it will not be denied.

"But in here? Yes, in here everything is truly and completely and totally awesome! It's a parallel universe of joy through reckoning! And I? I am your host with the most in this sunset and dark matter ghost town where wonders abound and the good life can be found roughly anywhere. So pull up a chair and prepare to have your minds, hearts, and souls blown open with my own grand imaginings—dreams taking wing from my mouth up south in the Motor City where we don't take your pity for a Gawd. Damn. Thing. I sure am glad you came and by the end of this broadcast or whenever they really turn the power out, I hope you feel the same. If not? No shame, no blame, my fame is potentially purely personal! I will not be offended if your bended little hearts can't bubble up with joy, I'm still your boy, Dawud B in the place to be, the dirty D!"

....

Dune first heard Dawud B by accident.

In the months of mass loss from the mysterious H-8 Syndrome, perhaps as a side effect of caring for her loved ones as they died, Dune had come to find comfort in the radio. Not for useful information, because that hadn't come in months.... It was just the sound of other voices—Dune had needed to hear voices that didn't need her, and didn't judge her, and ... were alive. She was turning the dial amongst the news stations, looking for the a cappella rhythms of conversation, when she heard him. Her fingers went still.

Dune had avoided evacuation for weeks, making a world of purpose inside her home, living by sun and moonlight, occasionally sneaking around to restock from the storehouses of foods she'd scavenged, harvested, processed, and hidden in her neighbors' pantries and freezers.

Winters used to be so bitter—she remembered weeks of snow days, she remembered ice storms and blizzards. The season was much milder than it used to be; each year the window of below-freezing temperatures shrank drastically, resulting in less snow, more sun. Her mother, Kama, the first casualty of the H-8 virus, used to alternate between calling this "the golden age of global warming" and telling Dune how the floods would precede an inland sea—"We gonna be Northern Cancun before it's all over." Maybe, someday. Winters now were wet—marked by sideways rain that cut like ice, and snow that didn't commit to the ground.

Remembering Kama when she was vibrant and funny moved a sharp blade of longing along Dune's jaw. She didn't want to be forcibly evacuated from her home. She didn't think she should wander too far from the place where she had last touched her mother, she might find herself altogether rootless. She was learning the conditions she could survive—in half a year she had learned how to accompany her mother through a fast, slow death; to keep her grandmother alive until she died naturally in her bed; to harvest, preserve, and store her own food; to map, study, and cremate the dead; to scavenge a ghost town; she'd even begun to believe, just the tiniest bit, in magic.

She kept living, each day layering itself over her skin in a way that felt like, but wasn't, purpose.

What Dune didn't know is if she could survive the loneliness. What she missed was different from company, from just having other humans to be around and talk to. She felt the loneliness that comes from being unwound from the superstructure of humans and their rhythms, the howling tunnel of being unknown in her inner thoughts, the madness of crafting all of her ideas with no one to critique, collaborate, or cheer her on. It wasn't sexual, it wasn't romantic. It was a quality of companionship she had never quite had as an adult, but witnessed all around her. Kama had had this with Brendon, and with Elouise, and other friends—people to fight with, laugh with, imagine with. Mama Vivian had had this too, a large community built up around her mind. Dune understood more each day why her grandmother had spent her last months staring at the wall, lost.

Dune needed a peer.

The radio reported that there was an Ebola outbreak spreading up the east coast. This made Dune feel unreasonable and jealous.

A known enemy.

The US Government was deadlocked—the conservatives in leadership were blocked by progressives at every turn, none of them doing anything that helped with the state of financial and psychological depression that was moving across the country.

She heard something about the Oscars and couldn't remember the last movie she'd seen, or when she'd seen something that wasn't a collapsing building, a rocking absent body, a wide empty road, wild pheasants in a precinct window.

People she had never heard of were battling with each other on social media, and that was reported as news.

The voices of the radio didn't know how it felt, this inertia, this genocide. She'd never known it before. But now, suddenly, this new voice, equal parts butter and gravel, a river rush of words with no hurry, static humming all around—knowing, knowing how it felt.

The need for human contact occupied her gut—heavy, pulling, quaking, unmooring her from her home.

As she listened to him, tears sprang to her eyes, pulled forth by his turbulent flow, his radical content, his proximity. As she listened to him she laughed, unclear if he was funny, or if she was just that grateful to hear a person who seemed to be thinking in the same disjointed way she was.

She couldn't turn him off.

When the show ended that first time, there was a moment of silence and then his voice came on again. It was the same two hour show, looped, and she listened to it, sitting still, swallowing it whole. She left it on as it looped through over and over again, had him with her while she processed food, managed the data on her grievers; she cleaned the house to the rhythm of his words.

When she woke up the next day she couldn't find his voice and she felt illogically crushed. Where was he?

This Dawud B must be within a mile of where she was. That's how those things worked, those mesh communications systems that covered blocks of territory. She had helped install an antenna on her home as part of Detroit Summer's radical DIY radio workshops. They cast their spells in a mile radius, two miles, max. Her lower back sent the little twinge that she recognized as the hope that she would find him in one mile, in one day's search. She reached back and gave herself a little massage, mapping the neighborhood in her head, the route she'd walk to look for Dawud B.

There was another person alive, a person communicating, making jokes, easily speaking her language. He was awake and possibly with other people who were alive and awake, within walking distance of her.

She thought maybe she should brush her teeth.

....

It had been seven months now since the sickness came. A forever long time, measured by the complete change of her world.

Dune had always been a slender thing. These months had hardened and fattened her. She felt a different kind of strength in her body, even as she carried more pounds on her bones. Foraging food, making a graveyard puzzle in her basement, building pyres. What was that workout called?

What she had heard on the radio had shifted over the months. At first she was angry that no one was speaking about Detroit. But when they started covering the mysterious sickness that was H-8, it was in some ways even harder. No one knew what to do other than document that masses of people in Detroit were going into a near comatose state and never coming out. People were dying and the cause was unknown.

For seven months Dune had listened as Detroit's crisis was ignored, then became the world's central story, then a tragic and contained mystery, to now—a rarely mentioned blip of dead city on the national radar. She listened to the news with a numb heart. Up close it was both so much worse and so much more normal than the broadcasts could capture.

Most people never see a stranger's dead body outside of their televisions, don't see their loved ones as abandoned bodies.

There were no reports of H-8 beyond the border of 8 Mile, even though some people had snuck their sick family members out in the early days. Once the barriers were guarded, that became much harder. Those sick had not recovered, but it appeared nothing had spread.

Dr. Natasha Rogers, the doctor who had treated Kama in the first moments of sickness, was working on a theory that H-8 was

man made. Rogers had identified that the virus repressed serotonin to the point of absence, but she couldn't quite figure out
how it targeted Black people and why the result was so consis-
tently fatal. Dune struggled to follow the science during their rare
conversations, how the "localized presentation of symptoms indicated the presence of toxic microorganisms." In order to make the
case, the doctor was eliminating every other option. The facts flew
over Dune's head, but the possibility resonated with her heart-
ache. Someone might have been responsible. Someone may have
done this to Kama, to Elouise and Lou, to Bab, to thousands of
people. Black people. She knew this couldn't have happened in a
white city, though she couldn't explain that logically.

Detroit was swept clean down to its roots now. What could
become of this abandoned city, of the survivors?

chapter three

Captain and the Kid

Captain had paid for this set of teeth and when he remembered that, he would pop them out of their sockets and move them around, just to enjoy them. His face was sunken in around his cheeks, he swore, because he had blown his flesh out playing the trumpet just like Louis Armstrong.

"Boy, you *got* to see this one!" Captain sat at the picture window of the third floor of his house, sort of the attic, although he had taught Jizo that only rich people had attics and that this was just the upstairs room in relation to many downstairs rooms. Most of those downstairs rooms had been damaged by fire, but the back stairway was ok. This room barely had any singe on it and the radiator worked. It had been a while since Captain had officially lived in this house, but now it was their best option. Something was happening in the city that he didn't want any part of and this house was easy to overlook.

He prided himself on teaching the boy about being Black, even though the child was not solely Black but some hybrid of maybe

Black and white, or Native American like Captain's grandmama, or maybe other things.

He also taught the boy key lessons about being poor, even though as far as he could tell, the boy came from nothing.

Jizo came running into the room, full of beauty and life. Captain guessed the boy was maybe four years old. When Captain introduced him to people, back when there were people, he always said, "He came with no adults and he's extremely capable of surviving! You gonna want to keep him, but you can't have him!"

The boy's skin was a deep olive-brown tone, his hair a frizzing halo of brown and gold ringlets, eyes massive and green. He currently wore a princess dress with green pants and shoes that had never been paired before this wearing—a left Mary Jane and a right Converse, both possibly too big. He looked proud of himself.

"This one is a beauty!" Captain beckoned the boy over from the door that led to their makeshift bedroom and the kitchen. Jizo's jaw dropped in appropriate amazement and he sent a brilliant smile over as thanks to Captain.

Together they were facing a Detroit sunset, a range of ribbed clouds, a glorious pink against a shadowy purple gray haze. It had been gray all day, but the city had a miraculous habit of clearing the clouds just enough for the day's glory to show.

Captain had spent months teaching Jizo to admire the sky. Not for a specific purpose, but because it was the best thing about Detroit. "Might as well get some joy on it."

When they used to go out walking together, Captain would reach over and pause Jizo midstep and point up at a cloud formation, a coming storm, a hawk on the hunt, a clear expanse. Jizo would look up and make a face of accurate wonder. Captain would affirm it because that was what he most liked about the boy really, that sense of guileless wonder.

"Now listen boy." Captain's tone was serious, even with the twinkle in his eyes.

Jizo looked up expectantly.

"The shit seems to be slowing down. Significantly, based on my recon. Ain't seen no ghouls in about three weeks officially today. And all the king's horsemen stopped circling end of last week, though they may be doing a wider sweep, so still be careful."

Jizo nodded in agreement.

"However!"

Jizo's eyebrows went up with perfect listener's surprise.

"I think, strategically, that you could chance a grocery store now."

Jizo looked thoughtful, if a little anxious.

"Only if you feel up to it, course. This is not a complaint, everything you been bringing home has been just splendid."

Jizo's brow relaxed and a peaceful smile came over his lips.

"You ready for a history lesson young man?"

Jizo nodded enthusiastically.

If Captain were a guessing man, he would guess that history was Jizo's favorite part of their friendship. For Captain, it was the companionship.

He'd been married to his soulmate Delilah Winifred Winters for forty-three years before cancer had slipped her away from him in a single month in 2004. They'd loved through two wars, a recession, being flush, and being homeless. They'd loved through three miscarriages together and one child, Harold, who died at two months old; Delilah's spirit children. Since her death, he'd been trying to find out what could possibly be good about life beyond

Delilah, since she had been the very best thing that had ever happened to him. He knew there was no other woman that would ever give him that special sort of gut belly laughter and quiet midnight comfort. He wasn't looking for that.

But how did anyone survive without true love?

Jizo seemed like a good person to share this inquiry with because how did anyone survive without a mama?

....

When Jizo showed up a year earlier, Captain had looked right, left, up and down trying to figure out where the child's mama was.

He'd asked around, but no one had seen anything.

The child had walked right up to Captain outside of the Salvation Army down on Fort. Captain couldn't tell if it was a girl or a boy. The little one walked up like she, or he, had been sent over by his or her mama to ask for something; direct, focused. But nothing came out of her or his little mouth. Captain looked around outside the store, then stepped back inside. The checkout girl, managing a backed up line of disgruntled shoppers, looked at Captain like he was completely losing it when he asked to make an announcement on the intercom system, so he'd just walked around the store, Jizo trailing him. The space was large, but it was also pretty easy to see every adult in it. No mama, no papa, no aunty, no one claiming the kid.

Captain didn't like the attitude of most of the people behind the counter, but he guessed they didn't like him either, seeing as how they had to buy whatever he brought in because his friend Herb ran the place. If Herb was here, he'd help find the child's mama. Captain had walked back out the double wide front door of the thrift store with its steel bars, trying to figure out what to do.

"OK boy, listen."

The boy looked up, so Captain figured it must be a boy.

"The thing is, I wish you had found someone else."

The boy looked dismayed.

"No offense! No offense. I am just saying that because here's the thing: I got no woman now and a real creative living situation. I don't truck with the police. And I don't see anyone around here claiming you."

The boy looked around, his mouth turning up to one side.

"Where you come from?"

The boy just looked up for a moment, then looked at Captain directly, peacock feather lashes batting slowly over pink cheeks.

"Did your mama bring you here?"

The boy tilted his head to the right, his face blank as if the idea of a mama was new. Then suddenly he smiled at Captain and reached in his back pocket. He brought forward a rock and offered it up to Captain.

It was a beautiful rock. The generosity of this child, handing him the only thing he had—Captain felt so sad that the boy had no people and so happy that the boy had chosen him. Captain walked with the boy to the bus stop, slow enough to tell him stories the whole time.

"Up there's the Ambassador Bridge. Make that bridges! Now, only one of them crosses the river, but the other one is still something. It is a bridge between hope and jack shit."

Captain laughed at himself and the boy smirked.

"But the man who built those bridges, he has some old comic book ass name I can't remember now. But he owned the Ambassador Bridge that goes across. See it? That used to have the most trucks on it daily as any border crossing in the known world."

The boy's left eyebrow lifted.

"You don't have to believe me! Still true. And they was making so much money on all of those trucks paying the tolls that this dude wants to build another bridge. He tried to get the permits but everyone tells him no cause it's already making the air stank and fu—uh, messing up the streets. But he's a rich old white man! So he just start building."

The boy's jaw dropped in appalled shock and he furrowed his brow.

"I know! So that bridge just ends in the middle of the sky, that's how far he got before the Coast Guard stopped him on account of he didn't have the right to cross they waters."

The boy shook his head.

Captain wondered briefly how such a small child could seem to understand so much of what he was saying. He felt grateful for the company. The boy showed no distress about his current situation.

"They call me Captain. What's your name, kid?"

At this the boy's eyes went blank again. The child's hair was soft and curly and seemed to float around his head, blowing in the wind, even though Captain didn't feel anything but sun on the place on his head where his hair had given up.

"I tell you what comes to mind, because I do have to call you something. When I was in the war there was these little Buddha statues all over the place, like baby Buddhas I guess. Had the mala beads on 'em and candles lit, real sacred like. And one man, he told me they were Jizo Buddhas for children who need to get home. I think get home *spiritually*, but anyhow, you a child who needs to get home, period. And maybe you is a spirit child, how would I know? So how bout I call you Jizo? Til you tell me your name?"

Jizo smiled and nodded at this. He lifted his chest a bit, clearly pleased to have this name. That smile made Captain feel quite proud of himself. As they walked and smiled, Captain hoped that the boy's mama didn't show up too soon.

chapter four

Voices

After the 2016 election debacle, Kama had started listening to Fox News once a week, a calendared commitment. It whipped up her fury, but she wanted to stay in touch with what the other side was building belief around. She felt like her people had been punished for myopia.

Dune had made a concerted and overt effort to be out of the house for this listening, as it felt like pure hate speech and she couldn't justify giving it her attention. But in these quiet months she began to be curious if anyone had a different take or more information.

It was from the conservatives that she'd gathered odd and untrustworthy bits of information that weren't covered elsewhere.

Three months ago: "It is a *war zone* in Detroit tonight as citizens storm the I-94 blockade demanding to be allowed to leave the city! Murder City citizens are *shooting* at the National Guard—no casualty report *yet*, but if you look behind me you can see the—there, that glow. There are a number of fires raging across the city from what appears to be a rash of arson, they are *setting their city on fire*! And—now this might be sensitive for some viewers—we have heard that people are starting to *cremate* their own *dead*. It looks like an apocalyptic movie set out here tonight, America. It's *total* chaos and devastation."

Two months ago: "Tuning in today to Zombiegate exclusives for Fox News! Detroit is a city in crisis—again! After months of quarantine, with no cure for H-8 in sight, citizens are now being evacuated to quarantine extensions in Ann Arbor, Grand Rapids, and Kalamazoo. Since the National Guard started getting sick, no one can be expected to continue holding the boundaries from within. Now the CDC claims each person will be observed for two weeks for signs of the sickness and then released amongst us! Let's just say, two weeks isn't long enough in my book. Local officials, including Mayor Maria de Costa and her city council, were forced to evacuate today to Ann Arbor. No one would have to force me to leave a city where people were going comatose right and left but hey, everyone's different ..."

"Phil, play the clip from Mayor de Costa's office: 'We will do our best to evacuate all healthy Detroiters out of the quarantine zone. We are devastated to report that as of this Friday, we cannot continue providing care for those who are infected with Syndrome H-8 within the city limits. The CDC continues to work tirelessly for a cure. We are all grieving. We will heal together. Detroit will return, the phoenix will rise.'"

"There you have it folks, Detroit is done."

Two weeks ago: "The National Guard is holding a secure perimeter around the toxic landscape of Detroit, Michigan. But National Geographic has sent in a team to observe the emerging wildlife in the city—boars, mountain lions, bears, abandoned pets gone feral. Who knows what they will find, or if they will make it back out? There is a lot of fear of what this winter will do to the properties of the city, sitting empty. Will home owners return to burst pipes and infestation?"

From these reports, Dune had learned that there was, maybe, an armed resistance. And that the guard was pulling back. And that if she wanted to leave Detroit, it would just mean a two week quarantine. She had successfully avoided the "forced evacuation" crews so far and planned to continue.

In the dark she'd put boards across the front window and doors, and exclusively entered through the back alley. The wood didn't really keep out the cold, so Dune had put up Kama's "winter curtains"—Mexican blankets nailed at the corners, which helped keep the cold out. After Brendon's death they used these every other winter or so when Kama was overwhelmed by the idea of heat-sealing plastic wrap on the windows. Dune kept her lights off, choosing to work by candlelight only down in the basement, sometimes all night.

She was staying.

....

A week passed before she caught the next Dawud B broadcast.

Kama had read Octavia E. Butler's *Parables Duology* with an Afrofuturism study group, and after, kept a small emergency preparedness box under the sink. Dune had mostly left it alone, using the flashlight a few dark nights. It was too small a box to make much difference in one person's survival, much less three or four. Dune shook her head at this further evidence that her mother's intentions had rarely resulted in manifestation.

The most valuable item in the box was a solar radio, which

Dune had pulled out and charged all the way up to use in the kitchen. Since Mama Vivian had died, Dune kept her grandmother's old radio on in the basement, waiting. He finally returned with a mic tap.

"Come ye, come one, come all, come hard. It is the Everything Awesome Circus! This room I sit in is somehow infinite within, even though it fits in four walls no larger than a shed. And that is just the first marvelous magic. I am a gorgeous little nightmare, over six feet of strapping Black brilliance spouting poems and jokes for drinks and smokes and right now, I would kill all of you for a twelve-year Macallan—shit, last year's Tullamore Dew. Bring. It. On. Over. There are fourteen things that I miss most of all from the age of civilization: bacon, lube, fireworks, buses, innocent tap water. Um, um six is elephants. Seven is fractal conversations with my homies, belief in the government—even just a little basic belief! Shopping with money, a comprehensive sense of the future, dyeing my hair, Grindr, packed bars on a Friday night, church. And the thing I long for precisely is when there was church happening down the block and the choirs were crying out their hymns to Jesus, 'Come please us dear lord we are the ones you abhorred now forgive forgive forgive us!' And I would be laying in bed hung over, listening to all that church, and just loving every single one of my Black people. I miss *these* things most these days and it pays to give in completely—some moments to the rage, write off the page, be an operatic tragedy on a private stage. Because now? You are the content. You are the muse. You are the data. Slay it with me, 'I am the content! I am the muse! I am the data! We are our content! We are our muse! We are our data!'

"And because I make it a point to be honest with you even if I can't be true to myself, I will admit I am finding there is no sage, no sanctuary in knowing why, what, how the hell I am here. No wisdom, no learning, no mind, no mind at all. I am the empty minded, the clear headed, the vessel awaiting wine and, perhaps, the divine."

Dune felt breathless as she listened to the words tumbling forth from the radio, from this stranger's mouth. She could almost see him pacing around in some small studio, with a unicorn on one side, an elephant on the other, walking in the tiny circus, dressed in something small and red with a tall hat. She pictured him brown, lots of long locs everywhere, tall and skinny with a charming, effeminate face.

She felt pulled to him, a tsunami in the moonlight.

Tomorrow, she'd begin trying to find him.

....

When Dune's mothergrief was too intense, she would go into the office closet to see if her parents had any more surprises.

She had found small caches of printed photos with their negatives in folded bags from CVS. Pictures of Kama and Brendon young, in bright patchwork denim—Kama a foot taller and already thick; Brendon not yet dignified, but gorgeous behind his glasses. Pictures of them holding her as a baby. Dune standing in a diaper and Kama's most sensible heels. Dune gripped in the arms of a beaming Mama Vivian and so many pictures of them all with groups. Brendon always insisted that they were making history and better document it.

The agitation of Dawud B sent her back to the office closet where there were still a handful of precious and unopened boxes to explore. She pulled out a small box made of tin, held closed by an odd leather clasp. Fingering it, Dune realized Brendon had likely made the tie himself. He was so effective at unnecessary fixes.

Dune carried the box to the living room and sat down. Unhooking the ball of leather from itself, she opened the box to find a stack of envelopes. They weren't stamped, they had never been sealed, but each one held a letter. The first one was in her father's handwriting, to Kama.

Dune wondered over the ethics of reading the letter for all of one second before consuming it—she needed this, she needed them.

Future wife,

Yes, I'm scared. But not of forever with you. I'm scared of your family thinking I'm an abomination, of you losing them by moving towards me. I'm scared of that kind of thinking and clueless about how to build community, at least as I envision it, with people who think in such divisive ways. I am scared that I can't be enough family to fill the gap if they abandon it. I am scared that my mother will be a difficult mother-in-law—not because of you, but because she wants me to wait and parent later, study first. She might be the only reluctant Chinese grandmother in the West.

But I am also incredibly excited. Our baby begins a lineage that defies the racism and xenophobia and anti-Asian sentiment that you and I grew up steeped in. He will be a living protest against small minds and borders. He will have your face with my hair, or my face with an afro. He will be smart and we will raise him to be a warrior for our causes.

I know you are scared. But I also know we love each other, and if "the long arc of history is bending towards justice," then love is the force of that bending. So I'm not asking you to trust me, I am asking you to trust love. Trust that the love you feel for me can help you feel my love for you. Trust that we will have an abundant life in love. Trust that our love will help us do what neither of us has ever done— raise a wonderful son and claim Detroit for the people.

B.

Dune traced the B with her fingers, wondering if her father had come to understand she *was* his son. She'd never known he expected a boy, never known he was so romantic. She pulled the next envelope open, and where her father's handwriting had been a formal neat print, she now saw the barely legible cursive of Kama's hand.

B

Who taught you to write in poems? I can't say it like that. It's wild waking up in my mama house knowing I have our child in me. Feels like a boy, I don't know. I don't want to peek. I don't want to know anything but what it feels like to relate to this little guava. I can't even really imagine it, just feels like a big energy inside.

I'm so scared B, so scared. I love you more than anything, but I never expected to have to choose between my family and my man. I'm scared I will be ignorant around your culture, your family. I know you are patient with me, but the learning curve is not a game.

Are you scared?

luv K

Dune realized that the letters were in reverse order. She picked up the whole stack and held them against her chest, promising to relish each one and read them multiple times and thoroughly. She brought the tin box to the bedroom, placing them on Kama's side of the bed.

....

Dune had climbed to the top of an empty four-story building, stepping over furniture and small creature bones and coffeemakers and other detritus in the stairwell. The cool gray city was mostly below her—burnt, vacant, the trees naked, the ground icy white with black patches of road showing the most recent tracks of National Guard or evacuation paddies or whoever else was still occasionally traversing the miles of empty road.

The wind seemed to slip through the glass of the windows, stealing into rooms, swallowing warmth. Cars sat still, mostly parked along the streets, there was order amongst the absence. It barely looked apocalyptic—or at least, not any more than usual. Detroit had looked like a living crisis for these last few decades of her life.

Now, the city was missing its most dependable sign of life: the people.

Dune descended to Cass Ave and walked down to the deserted Children's Hospital, climbed to the sixth story, and slipped onto that roof. She could see further from here; the sun was a dull clouded ball to the west. She scanned the tops of the buildings around her, looking for the slender reach of a radio antenna. Instead, she saw various satellite dishes, phone lines, and cables she didn't recognize.

Frustrated, she descended.

She had to find him.

She walked home and opened a bag of jalapeño chips. She sat the radio next to her, its small antenna fully extended. This was her third time listening to this episode.

"It's Dawud B in the place to flee and I still believe it is the Everything Awesome Circus. Copyright infringements paid out to my toy box! My people, all people, any people at all. I miss and long for you, I love you, I need you. Where did you go, where can you be? This place may be a dangerous place, but it is such a beautiful place! There is wild chicory, lavender, sage, rosemary, and dandelion root growing freely everywhere I turn. There are houses to burn and lessons to learn. The skies here will make you a fetishist if nothing has up until this point. I declare this—as someone who has enjoyed many a leather bound tryst with a fist—the heavy hanging clouds that shroud the sunset are pivotal perspectives on the relationship between earth and space, this is the only place where the night bruises the dawn. I am so glad to be here, let's get it on. Tell me you love me, tell me you will be here in the morning, let us go porning, whoring, swirling into the dappled light of an urban night. These are the only four things that matter: looking into someone else's eyes, sleeping deeply enough to dream, saying exactly what you mean and being creative—by which I mean creating things and indulging in the creations of others. Both and, and, and ... That is it my friends. You might think that your life matters because it matters to other people, but I am sitting here in an empty city that was so recently full of people, some of whom were good, some who were doing everything they could to make this world a beautiful place ... and you know what? They were fucking erased. They were all erased. And here I am. And all I have really tried to do since I got here was plant seeds of joy and water them with laughter, in the shadow of disaster. In the fucking cold. That sounds ridiculous and corny and stupid and dumb but I gives no fucks. It isn't lady luck that left me here!

"If you can smile, do it now. If you can laugh, do it now. If you can let the part of the self in you that is made of light shine? Let it fucking shine, my friends. This may be the end. It may, at minimum, be the beginning of the end. It may be a pretend world that we have been living in and now, if shit gets real, how do you want to feel? How do you want to *feel,* my loved ones? How do you *want* to feel? Yes! Yes to that. Let's drink to that. Hell, the liquor stores are open until forever."

Dune walked to the front door, slipped back into her boots, stepped into the still outdoors. The loneliness and longing that Dawud B's voice evoked in her was magnificent. She hadn't felt such a positive yearning since long before her mama died.

She looked up at the gorgeous sky he had called her attention to. It had cleared in time for sunset, purple dominated everything else and the clouds were thick and moving fast, as if they wanted to carry their treasures away from this place. A summer sky over a wintry earth.

She wondered when he'd recorded that show. She looked left and right.

"Dawud B!!" she cried out.

"Daaaawwuuddd!! Daaawuuud B!!!"

Panic whipped up to the surface of her system and she didn't try to swallow it down. She needed this stranger. She needed to know where he was, to look into his eyes, to breathe with him. She needed a friend.

She walked down off of the porch, past the sidewalk, into the center of the street. North was the Fisher Building. South were the round GM towers. Everywhere else was a shell, no spring in sight, just telephone wire and gravelly snow over pocked concrete.

"Dawud B, where are you??!! Please please answer me? Daaawuuud!!!"

The screaming became wailing, wild, desperate.

"Dawud pleeease!! Please please please please just answer me. Where are you!! Say where you are, I'll come find you. Just say where you are ..."

Her hands were reached up and out when she noticed them. She let them drop. Her shoulders felt weighted, like she carried collapsed wings. She dragged herself back to the house and sat down on the stairs just inside the door.

She had left herself too alone. She felt the solitude in a new, louder way, exposed to this wondrous voice, this person who was so clearly not sick, but not so sane that he had left. He was here. Was he here? Maybe he was just looping, a programmed broadcast, an algorithm. Maybe he had left long ago and she was longing for a human equivalent of starlight.

She missed her mama.

She missed too many people to even pull everyone into her heart at this moment. She was bent over on the stairs, tears and snot and spittle spilling through her hands.

She was saying Dawud's name for a while, but then she was saying mama, mama mama mama over and over again, a child who could not reason herself to a quiet place.

How could *her mama* be gone?

How could her mama be one of thousands of people who were no longer here because of ... of what? A fucking virus? A random variant? Why?

"Take *me*. Take me take me take me. Fucking take me!"

Dune leaned against the banister, grabbing the round wood with her hands, pulling herself against it with all of her strength. She held on, drowning, clasped against the edge of a boat in a storm. She longed for the relief of death. She wept until she felt nauseous, until she couldn't breath, until she saw sparkles at the edges of her vision and her eyes swelled and she had to cough in order to clear the tears from her throat.

She cried while the day turned to night, while the seasons changed, while the world went quiet and cold.

Whoever this was, this Dawud B, he had to account for this. He had to sit and face her and the swell of emotion he had evoked in her by being so alive amongst the dead.

chapter five

Loneliness

The sun glared into the room, cutting across the space to the massive rosewood dining table where Dune sat staring into space, her mind meandering all around. It wandered to a memory of Marta, a very specific time when Marta had touched herself in the passenger seat on barely-a-roadtrip to Athens, Ohio.

Dune couldn't remember what awaited them in Athens or whose car they'd borrowed, but the details that slipped up were well worn.

Marta had been in the passenger seat wearing a short feathery skirt and she'd propped her foot up on the dash so the wind whipped it up.

It was a joke at first, Marta rubbing her fingers suggestively along the outside of her cream colored drawers. Marta had been making goofy, over the top faces, and Dune laughed while looking around to make sure no other drivers could see.

Then Marta had started to enjoy it, evidenced by the tentative look of worship on her face, the growing damp mark of her pussy on the silky fabric.

Dune remembered Marta sliding her fingers down inside those panties while telling Dune to watch the road. The peripheral shadow and motion of the fingers there, the mystery of it; the wet thrusting sound.

Dune had driven a bit awkwardly with her left hand, using her right to fondle Marta's breasts until Mar came.

The memory brought a quick presence of desire into Dune's body, a pulsing. She touched her own breasts, found them hard and tender. Then she stopped. She couldn't do this here.

She stood up and walked to the living room, the desire growing in her. Not here. She walked past Kama's room without a thought, up the stairs, seeing the door to her own room, which she only visited occasionally these days.

She closed the door behind her, not wanting Dog as a witness. Dune was frantic. She pulled her shirt up and caught it with her chin, pulling the soft jersey of her sports bra down and flicking at her nipples, already tense with need. She rubbed two dry fingers over each one, then wet her fingers again and again, willing them to become suckling mouths.

She pulled down her sweats and stood in the pile of them, pressing spirals against her clit through her boxers, pulling her right nipple with her left thumb and finger.

With a small grunt she dropped to her knees, pressing up and up into her own rhythms, a sound slipping from her upper register as tremors released through her.

Nut, busted.

It had been months. She slouched to one side and then lay down, curled up in a ball. She shivered between laughter, crying, and quiet, and eventually slept a while, right there on the floor.

....

"You think I should cut my hair?" Dune was talking to herself in the bathroom mirror.

No one answered.

"I'm never going to find a husband like this," Dune said, then laughed out loud at her joke.

She hadn't done anything to her hair in months. A set of locks had formed in the back, a haze of frizzing curls around the front. Her mouth felt filmy. She'd been drinking too much, sipping at all different hours. Structure was becoming more and more slippery each day.

Sometimes she came to and realized she had been standing or sitting and just staring at the wall.

She'd wished, more than once, to be taken by the sickness, freed from loneliness. She could no longer imagine herself anywhere else; a massive blank filled her mind when she tried to imagine crossing the boundary of 8 Mile, sitting in a quarantine camp, joining into life again as if this wasn't the epicenter of her world.

Dying in some other random way.

"Fine, you know what? When the time comes, I will just cut it all off."

Dune stood up and opened the fridge. She was teaching herself to make bread because flour, salt and little yeast packets were some of the most resilient ingredients in the city. She had a bowl in the fridge with a ball of dough tucked tight in the center. She pulled it out and brought it to the table. She got Kama's favorite apron from the hook in the hall. It was from Ghana and seemed to have every color known to humans woven into it.

The apron felt too big to Dune in a way that had very little to do with size. She was bigger than she'd ever been, but still felt little relative to the space Kama had occupied. She could feel the grand scale of Kama floating out around her, an aura of absence. Blackness. Kama's incomparable Blackness. Dune felt washed out, these colors quieted around her where they had popped against Kama's skin.

Dune had traveled with Kama on international justice trips to Ghana, Kenya, Ethiopia, and other places on the continent, first as a baby on her mother's hip and then as a well-behaved kid who was easily entertained by books during meetings. Dune had always been aware of the eyes on her that implied some betrayal, some suspicion. Why was she so pale? What did she have to do with Africa, with this whole massive place and its million histories? This judgment also came through in teasing, playful words that all meant white—*obruni, gringa,* white girl.

Kama had defended her daughter's Blackness, her African-ness, but it didn't much matter. The cultural gap was so big and Kama walked with it like an open wound, heightening the pain of American racism with the knowledge that *Black people never even wanted to be here, now we fit nowhere.*

Dune had wondered a few times over the past few months if her multiracial background might be part of why she was still alive. It hurt to even consider it and she knew the thought was on the conspiracy theory end of things. Mama Vivian lectured in her head, "race isn't biological," but Dune's intuition whispered that this virus was some form of biological warfare. Whenever she slipped down this path, she would eventually stop and shake her head, ashamed of that little *National Enquirer* voice building its crazy narrative.

Dune knotted the apron at her back and then pulled a fist full of dough off of the cold pliant ball and tossed it back and forth, sticky between her hands. She needed more flour to do this, so with her free hand, she grabbed the blue ceramic canister off of the counter. Soon, there was flour everywhere, picking itself up in the air and flying around. Too late, she remembered that she needed to turn the oven on. She rolled her eyes.

"You are not a master chef. Where is it, about a woman never learning to cook or sew?" Dune turned the oven to 450 degrees. She put a small empty metal pan on the bottom level to heat up with the oven. Then she waited.

While she waited she found herself singing a song. She didn't recognize it, it moved out of her mouth like a butterfly out of a cocoon. Something new and fully formed.

I think too much about how I will die
It's the reverse at the back of my eye
It's the obsession I can't live without
It's the still comfort inside of my doubt

I think too much about how I'll still die
Even though I escape every day
All of this practice won't win me the game
I am a die-er and you are the same

It felt like a children's learning song. She shimmied the dough into the oven, then hurried a cup of water into the hot pan beneath it, slamming the oven door to steam seal her bread. The song kept coming.

My death is the soft voiced mystique of my dreams
She tells me her love's not as sharp as it seems

She says when it's time I'll beg her for relief
But I know she's a liar, I know she's a thief

She scoops out life, her hand like a sieve
Leaves droplets behind, which we mistake for gifts
I know the old souls who want to be whole
They hang from my hip, they won't let me go

The song evoked a stillness. It felt like the song was moving through from another place and the next part required all of her. She threw her head back, she let the song out.

I am the basket, I am the case
I am the only one left in this place
I should take action, take some offense
I should make babies, I should make sense

But I think too much about how I will die
Such tender violence I can't help but cry
I blow into dust, I burst into sky
But I don't want to know how, I want to know why

When the song finished, Dune stood quietly, letting breath return, landing back in her body. She felt like she had been a bit possessed, all alone in this place, but not quite alone. The song felt so good, and so true. Now the tune echoed in her head and she picked it up again at the first line.... *I think too much about how I will die.*

She sang the song for hours.

Then, because it felt good, she sang it for days.

....

The pond in front of her is glassy and calm, and her feet are dark and wide and unfamiliar, moving just under the water as she sits on the edge of the dock. She's never been here before, but it feels like home. Her dead husband comes up behind her—she knows the soft shuffle of his steps, she remembers grieving that sound. She listens as he slips out of his shoes, rolls up his pant legs and pauses just behind her before dropping down and scooting up to the edge. She is scared to move, to breathe too loud, or turn towards him, see him, speak. If he disappears, it will be that familiar grief that nearly swallows her whole each time. But if he doesn't, then she may be dead. And she can't be dead, not yet.

He starts speaking. His voice is the voice she knows, the rhythms she longs for, the sentences tentative at first, and then assertive. She softens, hearing him. She still doesn't turn towards him, she just watches the light move across the water's surface, reveling in the sound of him. He is telling a story, he has his teacher voice on. She can't understand a word.

After some time he is quiet. It isn't until he stands up and gets ready to leave that she turns to peek at him. His hand pulling on a shoe, the side of his face with that perfect hollow of cheek, his hair in a long black braid down his back, everything she sees is her love. As he walks away, she wants to follow, she wants to learn his language. But her feet are now a part of the pond.

chapter six

Anyone Out There?

"You are not dead! You are wonderful, one of the delectable leaders of our post apocalyptic metropolis, and don't you forget it. Because if we forget ourselves there will be no one left to remember. You are the ember that remains of the great vroom vroom of this motor city pity party and! You. Are. Precious. And where do precious people belong? On the stage! This is the age of the fantastical, it is time to rage, rage against that good night, because the dying light is sparkling snowflakes all around us, a million unique deaths are being died, a million protectionist fibs are being lied, and that's all somewhere out there. But we, my friends, are locked inside the Everything Awesome Circus! This is no one's freak show, this is the real can't-look-away resilient forest of the soul, stardust on our lips and hula hoops on our hips and Detroit on our tongue. We are alive, we are alive and we are young. We are the second line dirge unsung. I don't say 'we' metaphorically, *we* in here, you and me and the whole minstrel show. In a Black city you have to wonder, do only the maroons survive? Can the hhhhhwhite thrive? If anyone else is out there and alive, give me a call!"

He gave no number. He never did.

As Dune listened to him, she found coconut oil under the sink and twisted it into her hair with glistening fingertips. Showering this morning she'd noticed the hair growing under her arms, thick on her legs and between her thighs. The hair closest to her head was still damp when she pulled on a thermal, leggings and black cargo pants liberated from National Dry Goods, even a clean hoodie. She tried to remember the last time she'd been so clean.

Probably the last time she and Marta had loved on each other. She'd always been like that, more vigilant about personal hygiene based on the proximity of a sexual encounter.

Now the idea of just seeing someone who wasn't sick and wasn't in shock was a titillating possibility. She needed him to be real, that's all. She set her mind on it: either she was going to find him today or acknowledge that he was a figment of her imagination.

She looked out her window, up above the street, facing the strange silvery skyline of Detroit, the empty casinos, arenas, and office silos emerging suddenly from the brick and wood houses of the Corridor. All those buildings looking down with a million glass eyes, giving the appearance of a city with people in it, a city that could watch.

She knew different. There might not be another sentient soul between her and the river just beyond those shining empty towers.

"These days there are so many ways to sell yourself down the river. I have nothing but compassion in my heart, dear farts, but even after all this time I just can't forgive him—what did he see looking at me that struck him so dumb with wonder? Or was it the grief that made him believe there was nowhere to go but under? He was awesome, we was awesome, right here in the Everything Awesome Circus. The dog, the cat, the fat bat and the ally rat and ...

"Fuck. Anyone out there?"

Dune smiled. Yes, yes someone is. She zipped up another fleeced hoodie, pulled on fingerless gloves, then her mittens, then her coat. She stepped out into a white world. Was this the blank canvas developers had long dreamed of?

Evacuation trucks were still patrolling in the daytime. Or rather, one wheezing van was still making rounds. She'd layered the city maps in her head with a grid of back alleys and shortcuts to get around until it was no longer necessary. They'd give up eventually, definitely by February.

No one spent February in Detroit unless they had to.

chapter seven

Dangerous Adventures

Jizo was running north with Dog up a long alley that crossed five or six streets on the way to Warren. He had found a family pack of pork sausage burritos in a freezer. When he'd come out into the night, Dog was waiting for him. With no hesitation, he set the burritos down and hugged Dog, and Dog allowed it, his tail thumping the step. It was cold enough that their breath formed into a cloud between and around them. When Jizo was finished hugging and rubbing Dog, he retrieved the burritos as Dog stood up and took a few steps in the direction of home.

They started out walking and then Jizo tried to get a couple of steps ahead of Dog. Dog wouldn't allow it and the game had turned into an all-out race. They were running and the boy was laughing, a small breathy sound, as they came out on Canfield.

Suddenly an engine revved and lights flooded them both. Adults stepped out of a vehicle a half block down, with large and frightening gas masks on their faces. "Freeze! Hey! Michigan Militia—you are in violation of the city curfew!"

adrienne maree brown

Jizo froze for a moment, gripping the burritos closer. In an instant, Dog transformed into a fearsome beast, growling and gnashing his teeth at the car.

Then, as if responding to the same internal "go!," Jizo and Dog took off sprinting back down the alley. They heard the shouting behind them and then the van squealing into motion after them. Just before it turned into the alley, Dog pushed Jizo hard into a smaller alley behind a brewery. They ran through the thick smell of yeast all the way to 2nd and then swerved right. Dog led them to a porch with an opening on one side and they slid under it, safe behind the latticework. A few minutes later they saw the car drive by slowly, pausing at each street and alley before continuing.

Jizo thanked Dog with gentle petting, pulled up his hood and lay against Dog's side. He could nap for a short time in the cold and when he woke up he'd make his way home.

. . . .

Dune was in Kama and Brendon's closet again, on her knees. She was tired of reading, tired of organizing food, tired of exploring, tired of all the things she could do alone. She figured organizing the house was a legitimate activity.

But she wasn't organizing anything, she was just going deeper and deeper into the magical storage of her parents' remnants. Technically this could have been a walk-in closet, but from the day Kama and Brendon had moved in, it had been so packed that there was no room for the human explorer. Now, with familiar boxes already pushed out of the way, in this back corner of the closet, Dune had found something intriguing.

Stacked against the back wall were four green duffel bags, the

ARMY brand in big black letters down the sides. The bags were designed to open on one end with a drawstring that could be covered by a locking flap. There were straps along one side that could make the bag a long backpack. Under the flap of the first bag Dune reached was her mother's full name—Kama Tutashinda Chin. Checking, Dune found that the other three bags were for herself, Brendon, and Vivian. Mama Vivian's bag was a fresher shade of green, but otherwise the bags were identical. Dune dragged the one with her own name on it out of the closet and sat in the middle of her mother's floor with this treasure.

Pulling the bag open, she found a large gray tarp tucked around the top. Smart, she thought—that would help protect everything inside from whatever weather they moved through. Next was a towel the size of a sheet, made of a thin, light microfiber. Then a flashlight, a 28-pack of AA batteries, and a box of water conditioning tablets. A small book with maps of the Midwest, a zine on Camping with Kids, and a folding laminated sheet with campfire recipes. Then Dune came to a bunch of mysterious rolled packages.

The first package, when unrolled, was cloth diapers, old fashioned with large safety pins holding them together. The second package, wrapped in a cloth diaper and rubber band, was several sealed packages of baby formula. Dune realized what she was holding a second after the tears started running from her face. Her parents must have packed these when Dune was an infant, perhaps even before she was born. She kept pulling things from the bag: two empty baby bottles, a zippered canvas bag full of children's Tylenol, bandaids, alcohol, and a thermometer. There were two children's books, *A is for Activist* and *Earth Mother*, both clearly well loved and used. There was an envelope under the books, thick and sealed. Under the envelope was a ziplock bag with cash in it, maybe $200.

"Mom."

Dune was a summer storm, weeping with joy in sunlight. She wasn't sure she had ever felt so ... considered. Her parents were always trying to save the whole world. She hadn't ever articulated to herself what that felt like, but now as the feeling uncoiled, she realized she had often felt like her parents didn't have time for her. They loved her, of course. But in the heady world of leftist politics, she hadn't felt they had much time to think of her small and mundane needs.

Now she imagined Kama pushing Brendon to put these bags together, probably in an afternoon. Perhaps she had gotten the original three bags and he'd insisted they add one for his mother, sometime later? There was no way of knowing.

Dune wanted to tell her mother how different this apocalypse was from the one Kama had imagined they'd have to survive.

Slowly she stuffed things back into her bag, the envelope still sealed at the bottom. She'd leave it as long as she could, each chance for a new experience with her parents so precious. The whole bag was tucked back into the closet, on top of Mama Vivian's bag.

Laying on the hardwood floor of Kama's room, Dune pulled her knees up against her chest, then rocked until they fell to her right side and then her left. As she stretched her back, she imagined her mother, young and full of Dune, earnestly reading science fiction, prepper guides, maybe even climate studies. Knowing Kama, she had read with a notebook nearby, making a list of what her family needed, and sending Brendon to go get it all. Dune had often shirked away from the stories Kama and Brendon shared of their young life, daunted by the idea of them as romantic creatures. By the time she wanted to hear everything, Brendon was gone and Kama had often been too tender to talk about him.

But here she had a new kind of data—her parents had been prepared to survive, with her as a baby in tow. They were ready to carry a whole duffel bag for her and for Mama Vivian. They had considered her. They had a plan to try, a plan to live.

Dune felt some relief in her spirit, a strong sense that she was pleasing her parents just by persisting.

....

She was standing in the front hallway, feeling like a giant. She needed to reach her child, she needed to yell, but she couldn't. All the way down the hall, her daughter sat at the kitchen table, passed out, cheek against the wood. She couldn't move down the hall, couldn't get closer to her child. Instead, she picked up a stone from the bowl of blessings. She held the stone to her mouth, whispering into it: "precious, precious, precious."

Down the hall, a large Black man, a stranger, stepped up behind her daughter, sat at her table. She saw the whisper of a smile as her daughter woke. The kitchen became so bright she couldn't keep looking, and turned away, accidentally catching herself in the hallway mirror.

Her face was Kama's face! Kama's warm, sharp eyes looked back at her. But ... but she was still Dune, looking. Looking through her mother's eyes, at her mother. Kama reached her hand towards the mirror, and Dune watched the hand come closer, even as she watched her own motherhand extend from her body.

Dune jolted awake, covered in sweat.

....

The National Guard had padlocked many of the party stores downtown in the name of protecting the property and produce. Dune wondered if it made the owners feel safe, to know that food was rotting, bursting with worms and bugs behind locked doors.

The Guard had taken over the distribution of food from city volunteers shortly after implementing the quarantine, in part because only weapons could keep the growing hostility at bay. They'd handed out food packets and three-sip plastic water bottles that they brought in themselves, perhaps in response to an early theory that local meat or dairy was the source of the sickness. When they'd left, they'd taken their food and water, but left the locks.

Dune had done good work in the fall and, technically, didn't need anything else, didn't need to risk being seen. But there were things she wanted, liked, and missed binging on. Foraging was her new habit, more about passing the hours than feeding anything but her pain.

Plus she'd found Brendon's boxcutters with the tag still on them. And, she thought, fuck the National Guard.

The first store she'd broken into was Juke's Fresh Market, almost at 8 Mile. She watched it several nights over the course of two weeks. She didn't see any security looping these streets. The front was really well boarded up, while the back door just had three padlocks on it. This gave her the impression that the owners cared more about the glass than the perishables. This part of town was completely empty now.

Dune broke in through the back door around 3 in the morning, her nose covered in a lavender-oil-drenched bandana to block the smell of produce left to its own devices. The stench penetrated her bandana—it was much worse than she'd expected, so bad that she got scared there would be a bunch of bodies when she got all the way inside. But it was just the meat counter and the produce. Dune wondered why they had left the meat like that? Had Juke himself gotten sick?

There were flies, roaches, and worst of all, rodents inside, unfazed by wood and padlocks. They flitted and scurried near her, and she made loud noises with the box cutters against the shelves. Dune felt some pride in her ability to keep moving forward—before H-8 even one pellet of mouse poop would have made her abandon the mission. The rats had burst open bags of rice and grain, cookies, crackers, ruining and devouring many of the foods she was interested in. The freezers were still on, though, casting an eerie light through the store. Dune was able to get big bags of frozen berries, waffles, hot pockets and enchiladas. She was also lucky with jars and cans—red lentils, canned beans, canned fish, canned pickles, honey. She found a shelf full of dog food in cans, and even a few bags on upper shelves that hadn't been disturbed. The score, though, was toilet paper. She grabbed enough toilet paper to get her through to next summer.

When she'd finished loading up the car, she arranged the padlocks so that the door still looked locked. She drove home with the lights off, feeling alert and grateful. At home she added Juke's to her notebook as a place she could return to for frozen food. She also added a large Lego to the model. It pleased her to add a place that had no death to it.

She wasn't only searching for Dawud B, or for food—Dune needed community. She found herself drifting further away from the city center, stealthy and alert, wishing she could get lost. The houses out here had been abandoned with intention and protective reluctance, windows and doors boarded up, bright yellow "Evacuation Participation" stickers on the doors.

Bodies that had been left behind in the first wave of evacuation were in various states of decomposition now, depending on whether they'd been left in a home with heat, open or closed windows, pets, security systems. The smell was unmistakable—Dune found a gruesome comfort in the fact that in death everyone smelled the same. Rich or poor, skinny or fat, every race, every religion, every person she discovered in the process of decomposing went through the same foul process.

This was meant to happen in the dirt. Dune understood this now: a human body is meant to nourish the soil, to be pulled apart by a system of bacteria and insects and creatures who can swallow the body, change the body, and make the body into food for the earth. This gave her a small sense of peace inside her grief, this idea that there was a natural arc towards death, sometimes in individual moments and sometimes in mass sweeps through the population. It was devastating for the heart, but generally good for the earth. Even with the stench, which seemed to embed itself in the walls and carpets, passing through the glass of windows, sliding under the slim gap of doors. As soon as she smelled it she would make note of the address and the date she had come across this death, making a black flag with no name for the model. For now, these were her unknown soldiers.

....

The gun was pointed at her midsection.

Building off her success at Juke's, Dune had made a two-hour evasive journey across town in her stealth dark car to the Krogers by Southfield, avoiding a pack of wild dogs who were owning an intersection and maybe having a fight.

She had only watched the Krogers for one night and it looked abandoned, no signs of life. Dune had come back on this quarter-moon night to make the most of the dark. It was a perilous journey, one she couldn't afford to do too many times. She'd cut the single back padlock, jimmying open the door. She had her mind set on rice and quinoa that hadn't been claimed by rats. She also wanted some more pizzas, maybe some frozen burritos, if she was lucky.

But someone with a gun was here before her—had taken up residence in the place. It was so smart, claiming a grocery store for a home. She couldn't help but admire the forethought of this person who might be about to put her out of her misery. It looked like a very skinny man, wearing layers of clothing and scarves. He had on a shower cap and a cat eye mask that sparkled.

Dune pulled her hat off slowly, so he could see her face. She was afraid.

"I didn't know anyone was in here," she offered quietly, wanting him to hear that she was willing to be in the wrong.

"You with the government?"

Dune shook her head. She hoped that was a point in her favor.

"What you need?" The gun didn't waver. "You got cash?"

"A little." Dune kept one of Paulie Vereen's bills on her, more with the idea of bribing a guardsman than purchasing high snack food. "Pizza. Maybe some frozen meat? Brown rice. Quinoa?"

"Ki-what?"

"Grains." Dune had her hands wide, at her sides.

"Aight, this way." The gun moved, gesturing her deeper into the store. Dune felt a small shiver of self-preservation then. What was she thinking? This guy could rape her, kill her. Eat her. She had her back to the door.

"Actually, I'm good." She took a step back and the gun paused in the air.

"You don't trust me, a total stranger?" There was a smile there, the eyes gleaming a bit in the shadow. "Man, I'm not sick. I'm … I'm not gonna hurt you. We don't eat meat, so there's a lot of frozen meat here."

Dune felt genuine confusion. She should leave. She was facing down a handgun as an unarmed and generally non-violent person, unskilled with a weapon even if she had gotten her hands on one. All she knew how to do was put people who were already dead into her fire. She felt humbled and on edge with the danger.

"No, really. It's ok. I'm sorry I bothered you." She took another step backwards. She heard a small curse and tensed to run.

He lowered the gun to his side and pulled off the eye mask to show a remarkably young face, a teenager. The shower cap came off, a head full of tight curls. The masked man had been menacing, the unmasked young Arab boy in front of her looked as scared to kill her as she was to die.

"Give me a couple minutes?" He slipped away and Dune stood there, focusing on her gut, trying to get a clear read. She felt ok standing still, but not following him.

He returned in a few minutes with a stack of frozen supreme pizzas under one arm, two massive bags of brown rice under the other, and a grocery bag full of frozen steaks and ground beef. The gun was nowhere in sight. She passed him the $100. He passed the food to her and let her go put things in her trunk in a couple of trips. Once he had handed things off he pulled his cat eyes back down over his face.

"Cool. This is our place," he said quietly. "Me and my family. Don't come here again, ok? If it wasn't me ..."

Dune understood. She was lucky. She nodded with gratitude to the boy, wishing they could be friends. "Stay safe," she offered.

"Stay alive," he responded.

The gun incident was clarifying. The next morning, before dawn, Dune liberated an Emerson bowie knife from the hardware store. What if that boy had told her to get on her knees? If he had ordered her into a back room? She'd been lucky. She carried the knife when she left the house now, just in case.

chapter eight

Dawud

Dune could not tell if she was going mad or already there.

"And isn't that the point?" she said aloud, her favorite way of talking to herself these days. "I wouldn't be able to tell. And that is why we are looking for a man from the radio."

She had her radio piped into her right ear, standing on John R. near Mack, across from a building she had passed a million times in her search for Dawud B, but never entered. It was the repurposed urgent care wing of the Detroit Medical Center; above the double doors was a cheap vinyl National Guard Crisis Center sign.

"No way. It can't be."

It was too close. There's no way he could have been this close all this time. And as far as she knew the Guard had left the city weeks ago.

Cowards.

Dune felt a wave of rage move up her. Or maybe it was anticipatory disappointment? Was Dawud B a fucking colonizer?

Someone who came to "save" the poor Black city from its woes? Had the Guard pulled out and left behind some incompetent spoken word artist as tribute? Had she spent all this time longing for the company of a ... a soldier?

"Focus Dune," she interrupted her internal rant. And then, "If you're angry, you're in the past." Was that Lao Tzu? "If you're scared, you're in the future. If you are talking to yourself out loud in an empty city about to break into urgent care, you're in the present."

The building looked abandoned, but there it was, a set of long slender antennae emerging from the roof, rigid tendrils of smoke signaling a presence, a communication.

The signal in her ear was the clearest it had ever been, Dawud B still going strong.

He might not be in there.

He might be anywhere.

"There is an elephant named Henrí, mid-rant, walking through my fancy pants bedroom right now folks. It's got trunk sized smokes, mouse sized jokes and a generally disgruntled nature, it smells of manure and by that I mean—cover your ears—shit, but someone seems to have dyed or tickled it bright pink a while ago. I am talking fuchsia—and I rarely say it because I loved each angsty hit but fuck Sia, fuck her all to hell, always a tragic songwriter never a celebratory diva, and I. Wanted. More. At minimum more face, I need to see that face! Now where was it, it being he, he being me, me being tickled pink by the big stinky gray face traipsing past my blue satin sheets, my friends? It's time to make amends because this elephant is angry as all hell because this right here, the golden land, the promised land, was supposed to be a good investment!"

Dune approached the building slowly. She never assumed she was unseen, unwatched.

She never quite felt alone. She felt more and more often that the city was watching her through gaping, longing eyes. She wondered, not for the first time, if the buildings of Detroit could feel what was happening, if they wanted the grief to come inside and fill them up, or stay out of their halls.

There had been 713,432 people counted here in the last census before the plague. Now, there are at least that many stories, of who stayed, who left, and how they died. Dune felt pressed between unspoken memories, too many new ghosts making the air thick.

"Ok my Wudites, my Dawuisms, my busy Bs—I have a song for y'all today, because I am a renaissance man, with Appalachian tendencies. It goes like this:

"Beware a hungry woman
You'll always wake up tired
You won't know how to please her
Her beauty knows no bounds"

His singing voice titrated between a flat grunt and a sharp caterwaul. Dune could feel what he was reaching for, a bluesy soulful old Black howl, but what came out sounded like it began in a throat wound.

"Beware an anxious woman
She'll bring her ghosts around you
You'll think that you can help her
She's married to her heart

"Beware a dreaming woman
Her feet don't love the pavement
She'll always need to wander
She's never coming home"

Dune saw herself in the side window as she approached the door. She looked normal, like herself, in a way that felt ostentatious. Too sane for this place. But in this city, empty save for people who have left all coherence behind, anyone who was dressed, clean, making eye contact, able to speak in full sentences, and stayed here, must be mad.

She wondered if Dawud B would realize that immediately and refuse her friendship.

Then she laughed out loud at the circuitous conclusion. That fucker was still here, too. Hopefully right here.

"Beware an angry woman
She'll see the flaw you've hidden
She'll razor it against you
Until there's nothing left

"Beware the grieving woman
Her tears will flood your hours
Her heart forever broken
Forgets a way to live"

Months ago, people had congregated at the crisis centers, seeking evacuation plans, sometimes leaving their sick people behind in the waiting room as an act of mercy or desperation. Because some people, even if they weren't sick, were allowed to go and others weren't. Dune would never describe the selection process as arbitrary, but she damn sure didn't know the logic.

She pushed through the first double door into the waiting room, stout white walls adorned with solid strips of horizontal blue paint that she supposed were meant to evoke order, a clear path through to health. There was a neatness to the whole space that slowed her breath.

The biggest sign that this might be a home to the living was the lack of bodies.

"Beware the witching woman
She sees the trail before you
Her love comes with a warning
She'll end you with a spell

"Beware the happy woman
She'll never really need you
She knows how vast this world is
You'll have to love yourself"

Dune crossed the waiting room area and peeked through the check-in window on the off chance there was someone in there courting appointments. Empty, but orderly. She inhaled and smelled something familiar—Marlboros? The only boy she'd ever kissed smoked those; she had a brief full-lipped memory.

She slipped to the right and listened through the rubberized double doors that led back into a massive space divided by hanging pale blue separator cloth, where people had been examined and diagnosed. She remembered coming here one morning with Kama, shortly after Brendon's death. She remembered sitting amongst a crowd of people coming down from their highs, people holding their hearts or bellies with strained faces, a pregnant woman pushing breath through pursed lips and insisting they wait on her boyfriend, who was parking—he was parking the entire time Dune and Kama were there. Kama, barely alert, had said she had food poisoning. Dune suspected her mother had overdosed on something and wouldn't admit it. Dune glimpsed her mother now, laying on one of these beds, on her side, eyes closed to avoid her only child's searching gaze.

A low mumbling pulled Dune out of her memories, her procrastination. She pressed forward. Sliding her feet, trying to be as quiet as possible, Dune realized she was a little afraid. Of everything. Of meeting Dawud, of him being horrible, or disappointing, or wonderful, or anything other than Dawud B, the steady voice on her radio. Maybe it was best to not meet him? Even as she thought this, her feet kept sliding forward.

It was bright—light pouring in through skylights and windows. This space had all the curtains pulled aside and the room she was in was full of cots lined up side to side. At the end of the slender walkway between cots and curtains was another set of double doors. She was moving slowly and had turned the dial down on the headset, but she could hear the synchronicity between the broadcast in her right ear and the growing murmur up ahead.

She paused at the doors and took a deep breath.

"Let him be a good, nice, normal person. Let him be Black. Let him not be a violent serial killer rapist fuck. Let him be real."

Dune eased open the doors and stepped into another long room. The room was tight with computers set on rows of collapsible tables, wires tentacled on and under every surface. The computers were an assortment of years, makes and models, all antiquated. Big heavy PC monitors next to sleek slender Macs, laptops, tablets. There were a few unused projector cubes, but they looked out of place in the time warp city.

Only one person sat in the massive, well-resourced room.

One whole person.

He looked familiar.

Dune honed in on the Black man. He looked at least forty, working on a computer by the wall. His eyes were closed, but his hand came up, pointing a gun at her, the tip tilted down a bit.

He had on the bottom half of a guard uniform, camo pants and boots, but his shirt was bright red and said "Cass Tech" in faded block letters. If he'd gone to Cass Tech, he was a Detroiter, at least. His head was mostly bald, a stylish little patch of hair lingering soft on the tip top. He was stocky, thick through the chest and belly, and still talking.

As she looked at him, a dissonance formed—she recognized him: It was the fucking sour-faced guardsman from the town hall Elouise had organized.

She cursed it. He *was* a soldier.

But how was that possible? Dawud B on her radio was the embodiment of a free thinker—he couldn't also be one of the sheep.

She walked down the row of computers until she stood in front of him, hands raised open at her sides to show she meant no harm. The gun followed her, but his eyes didn't open. She focused on checking out his technology—he seemed to have one of every kind of device in a half circle around him, with a map of Detroit above him, projected from his cube.

Now, slowly, his eyes opened. He looked at her with naked curiosity, his gun now resting in his hand on the table, his bulk leaning back in his chair. He still didn't seem to quite see her; he seemed rather to be looking into and through her.

"Well beautiful people, what can I say at this moment? Something truly rare has stepped into the Circus today friends, I can't pretend my mind isn't bending trying to comprehend what I am staring at right now." His face was wonderstruck, his voice sustained the drama. "A unicorn! A real live unicorn, absolutely majestic no shits no tricks. The horn, is it ivory? Flesh pure rainbows, shimmering like the proud mother of confetti at her wedding to glitter. It is time to go for a ride, I will be right back, or I won't. If you want to see the unicorn live and in person, just give us a call folks. Til then, keep it nonlinear!"

....

Dawud B flipped a switch, pulled off his headphones with his free hand and set them down slowly in front of him. Dune didn't know what to do with her face. He was alive, he was real. Possibly a pig. Aiming a gun at her. Not sane, not so far. But maybe that was a lot to hope for right now.

His eyes focused as he looked at her, until she felt like he actually saw her for the first time.

"Foe or friend?"

His look was too intense. She held his eyes because she was stubborn, but she wanted to look away.

"I heard your show. So. Fan?" She heard how disgruntled she sounded.

"Yeah?" Dawud chuckled then, soft cheeks dimpling. Dune didn't laugh with him, though a brief smile came involuntarily. Dawud lifted his hand to his mouth, a slender length of ash falling away from the cigarette as he sucked it in. Marlboro Red.

"I'm not sure why I'm here." Dune felt confused. She hadn't expected a soldier. It changed everything for her.

"Well, the universe only sends me things she doesn't understand," he offered.

Dune nodded, disoriented. She had searched for Dawud B with such a worshipful, groupie feeling, like there was only an autograph at the end of this exchange. Now she felt like she should be disgusted, even though he seemed nice enough. She started to innovate. "I have a lot of information. I thought maybe you could use it."

Dawud nodded, "Well. It's possible." He looked around the room, full of machines, empty of staff. "I'm pretty much the only member left on the group project around these parts. What kind of info you got?"

"Stories, I guess. What people are crying over, getting sick for."

Dawud B leaned in, indulgent skepticism on his face. "Let me guess, they talk to you?"

"No," Dune noticed the gap in his teeth, reminiscent of Elouise's smile. She hoped, not for the first time, that she wasn't putting Dawud's life at risk because she was lonely. "But I listen."

"OK," Dawud tapped his fingers against his lips. "You got these stories with you?"

Dune shook her head. "It's all in my basement. I live just down the street. I can bring pictures, bring the files over."

She actually wasn't sure she could do this, or if she wanted to. If he was working with the National Guard, he would most likely ruin everything. But maybe the show could be used to gather more stories, or share them. It felt fair to offer.

"Or I could just come there, no big."

"I hadn't considered that."

"Well what had you considered?"

"I don't want to be evacuated."

Dawud looked at her hard. "I'd have never guessed."

"If you're part of the National Guard, I mean. I've seen y'all rounding people up."

"Not my beat. Plus I think everyone else left."

"Why are you here?"

"Oh, you know, Detroit in winter is just irresistible."

They looked at each other for a minute, neither offering any ground.

"Ok, I won't evacuate you, scout's honor." He held his hand up, first in a soft salute and then a rock on sign.

Dune felt her gut settle and as that was the only thing she had to rely on at this moment, she trusted it.

"How come you didn't get sick?"

Dawud scoffed a bit and shrugged his shoulders, eyebrows high and wide. He waited for her to continue.

"I don't want to risk ... you." The words were so awkward that Dune's inner lesbian died a bit.

"Yet you came here." His tone was soft. "Look—other than doing the show, I've been basically sitting here playing Rubik's cube with data. And I never figured out how to get that shit to line up. I mean—is it dangerous, what you want me to see?"

"I don't think so. Have you been out of here much, interacted with sick people much?"

"Yes."

She looked up then, finally meeting his eyes again. They were quiet for a moment, and she felt him sizing her up, felt him clocking her soft boyishness. She felt pale, felt the fine dark hair escaping her braids as they reached down her shoulders. She'd worn a purple baseball cap with an Old English D on it, and wondered if she looked as cool as he did.

He reached some affirmation inside and stood up, pulling on a dark brown hoodie that bore a National Guard logo. With no apology or acknowledgment he tucked the gun against the small of his back. Dune made a mental note not to surprise him.

"Machines, if I don't come back, she ate me and you have to kill her." He smiled at her.

Dawud didn't seem like the magical poet on the radio, he was so matter of fact, so nonchalant. If she hadn't just seen him saying *Everything Awesome* things, she wouldn't have believed it at all.

Outside the center they fell into a quick pace as they walked between the alert buildings. Dune wondered if Dawud B felt the watchfulness of the city. A pheasant landed on the block in front of them, sporting a red chest so bright that Dune figured he was male, his striped tail sharp and long. Another landed, and another, all perching easily in the middle of the street. Dune wanted to tell Dawud that a group of pheasants was called a bouquet, but she didn't know him like that yet. Dawud spoke first, offering his hand to shake without slowing his pace.

"I'm Dawud Brown by the way. I grew up here in the Corridor and then we moved on up to Outer Drive."

Dune didn't say the obvious, *I know you're Dawud, I've been listening to you, that's why I came.* She pumped his hand awkwardly, answering, "I'm Dune."

"'Fear is the mind killer,' huh?"

Dune felt her shoulders soften a touch, as they always did around someone familiar with her namesake. "I've basically lived here my whole life. Except school. In Philly. We're going to my mom's house."

"Why'd you come back?"

"My moms was sick. Before all this." Dune had been forgetting this since Kama died; her mother's depression, her stuckness, her mother's inability to really keep going after her father died. She had unlinked these things in her mind. "Maybe she didn't really want to be here. I took care of her while she was here tho."

Dawud paused in his step. She kept walking. He caught up with her and she looked straight ahead, feeling his probing attention. Finally she snuck a sideways glance, shifting the interrogation: "Why *you* here? Where you live now?"

"Brooklyn, New York City. The National Guard put out the call to help with the quarantine and evacuation—I had to come."

"My mother considered the impetus to soldier an illness."

Dawud paused again, then stepped next to her. "Smart mom."

"But you're a soldier."

"Yes." Dawud walked a few steps, thoughtful. "I was young and we were broke. I wanted to go to college, and Jorge Rodriguez recruited me in high school, offered to pay my way through. It seemed like a useful set of skills to have as a gay Black man, a way to increase my safety, especially since otherwise I was a gay Black poet."

Dune nodded. She needed Dawud B, but she didn't trust Sergeant Brown. "Why did you leave Detroit?"

"Oh man, I love this place. Just couldn't make a living here or be myself—when I was younger anyway."

"I haven't been to New York since they built the dams. Does it feel different?"

"Oh yes. And no. I mean ... if you spent time near the water, it's different. It's kind of ... claustrophobic? If you ain't at ground level it's aight tho, or just moving through the streets, it just feels cramped like it always did."

"What do you do there?"

"Poetry." Dawud bounced himself up and down a curb, catching Dune's side eye. "I know. I'm good at it too. I'm impossibly talented."

"I don't know too much about poetry," Dune said, cautious. She knew she didn't like most poetry, especially not spoken aloud. The rhythms grated her, made her long for melodies. But for months she had loved listening to him.

"Me either!" Dawud laughed out loud. His laugh was loud, shameless. "Unfortunately it's how most words show up in my goddamn head! I also bartend sometimes."

Dune looked around, disconcerted as his laugh echoed through the emptiness. What if someone heard him? They were crossing Woodward, passing People's Records, heading between a dusty coffee shop and a boarded up bank. There was no one in sight, no moving cars, no people, no grievers.

When Dawud's laughter faded she could still feel it reverberating in her awareness, a rare sound. Dawud B, in the flesh, was walking next to her, laughing. She decided to savor it.

"What do you do?" She was grateful that he kept talking as if unaware of his impact on her. She never felt shy around guys, never felt moved by them in any way. Grief and desperation might be in effect, something primal and human, beyond labels. Mostly it was the feeling of meeting a celebrity, even though she was probably his only listener. She worked to rein in her awkward energy. He was talking to her, "What did you do, I guess."

"Oh ... Well, I cared for my family—my mom, like I said. She couldn't hold steady work. And my grandmother—she was just really old. I was applying for schools—grad schools. Was trying to decide between Philly and California, but ... I didn't really do much. Ran dishes at the Standard for cash. Moms just needed me around."

Dawud didn't mention his own life in response, which Dune appreciated. She wondered if he had a sense of what it was like to love a parent who couldn't be the caring one, how much work it took to run a household cloaked in grief.

"You live alone?"

Dune nodded, aware of the lack of fear she felt revealing this. "Yes. Now."

"Got it."

They crossed Cass.

"Almost there." She offered, then got quiet for a minute. "Dawud, have you ever killed anyone?"

Dawud stopped in the street and turned to face her. "Poetically, yes. Sexually, yes. But I have never taken the life of another human. And I struggle with killing anything else—I can't even stomp on roaches. Mosquitoes have their way with me. I am trained to defend myself if I ever felt my life was in danger and in those cases, I wouldn't use a kill shot. No blood thirst here."

Dune nodded at this, some unspoken tension softening.

"And you, Dune? Have you ever killed someone?"

Dune shook her head no, with a small smile at the very idea. She bowed slightly in gratitude for his answer, and he met her bow with a curtsy thick with flair. She turned and started walking again, a soldier at her side.

Dawud let her silence carry them past the overgrown yards, domestic ruins, the field full of upturned solar panels. These hadn't changed much during the plague, but they felt part of a landscape that had been waiting for just such a crisis to reveal their unkempt and true nature.

They turned onto Second Avenue. Halfway down the otherwise empty block, across from the three floors of the ornate old Coronado apartment building, sat Dune's big yellow house, the first floor windows and door boarded up. Dog came running around the house, like he'd been hanging out in the back yard. Dune turned to let Dawud know Dog was no danger, but Dawud was already smiling in recognition.

"Rudy! Whatchu doing here?" Dawud got down and pet Dog, hugged him. Dune felt comforted by this. Dog was vouching for Dawud.

She led them all through the gate and around to the back, which looked impenetrable with its boards and padlocks. Dawud looked away as Dune handled her maze of security, which she appreciated immensely. After a few minutes, Dune cleared her throat. Dawud turned around and she did an awkward welcoming gesture with her hands and a slight bow of her head. Dune wasn't sure where this clumsy physicality was coming from, but she definitely didn't know how to be around this human. She felt big and unwieldy and odd. She stepped in the back door.

Dawud followed her lead, pulling off his boots and coat in the back hall and hanging them on the wall, then stepping behind her into the kitchen. Even though she had been hungry for Dawud's company, Dune felt a hyper awareness of how unready her space was for a guest. The living room was full of her projects, books open for her research, her radio on the kitchen counter with Dawud's looped voice pouring out of it. This had been her solo sanctuary since Mama Vivian left her.

Dune moved quickly ahead of him to turn the radio off, but he made a humble and slightly embarrassed face anyway.

They stood cramped in the kitchen, which took up the center

of the house. He clocked the vintage cream tiles with golden appliqué, framed by dark wood and open shelves everywhere, with a big silver fridge, and sun pouring through the windows. And in the middle, the massive table.

Dawud started biting the fingernail on his left ring finger.

Dune was in charge in this space, taller as she stood in the kitchen. "What I want to show you is actually in the basement." She stepped back into the brief hallway, opening the last inner door to reveal the dark basement staircase. She checked that he was behind her and headed down. "Give me a minute, the light switch that works is down here. Once I get it on, come down. And close the door behind you," she tossed back over her shoulder.

He did so, stepping onto the top stair, his hand on the doorknob behind him, prepared to pull the door tight. The hot air blasted him. Dawud stood in the shadow for a moment, some premonition creeping over him in the near darkness. There was something in this basement that would hurt him, his skin goose pimpled in alertness.

He didn't know this woman from anyone. He was following her because she seemed kind, interesting. And he was tired of getting nowhere with this sickness. He touched the walls on either side of him as he descended. He truly hoped this wasn't some ruse in which he was about to be captured and eaten by a ravenous fan. But then again, at least that would be something new. "I'm not as delicious as I look, apropos of nothing."

At the bottom of the stairs, Dune laughed quietly as she flipped on the light. Dawud was transported.

The basement was one room that ran the length of the whole house, mostly finished. Filling it up, almost wall to wall, was Detroit.

From the floor to the low ceiling, the walls were papered with faces, actual photos printed on paper, not a projection in sight. The photos were incredible, up close full color portraits of people in various states of grief. Some of them bore torment on their faces, others looked numb and absent, some grimaced, some just looked exhausted. All of them looked down at the remarkably thorough physical model of the city of Detroit. Dawud had the brief and eerie feeling that he was glimpsing the ancestors watching over them.

Dune walked Dawud around the model until they faced Detroit like gods, or Canadians, seeing the city spiral up and away from them, from the river. Dawud looked at Dune for permission, she granted it with a welcoming hand.

He leaned close to the model and began to read.

There were creative replicas of various landmarks, along with all manner of toy houses from board games and constructs made of Legos, all structured around black cardboard highways and the blue scarf at their hips, the Detroit River. Most of the houses and structures in Dune's neighborhood had little sticks reaching up from them. At the top of each stick was a strip of paper with black numbers on it. A landscape of sandwich toothpicks. As Dawud looked closer, he noticed some sticks had multiple strips of paper attached. There were multiple spaces of vibrant green that looked like real grass and he wondered how she was growing things on the model.

His fingers moved over the landscape like he was dowsing. Without realizing he was looking, he found where he was from— Outer Drive at Nine Mile. There was a cluster of tiny red Monopoly houses. Dune followed his attention, wishing she could shift the tables a bit for him, so he could slip his larger frame close enough to read the strips of paper around the corridor. The tables had grown together, but Dune didn't know how to explain that to her guest.

His attention was on the northern edge of the model and, after a while of his finger drifting over the flags of mourning, his familiar voice began to speak the slips of paper aloud.

"1904 Outer Drive, November 2nd, #146. 1907 Outer Drive. November 2nd, #4. 1896 Outer Drive, November 3rd, #23." Then, "1956 Outer Drive. November 5th, #654."

Dawud cast Dune a raw look. "Number six fifty four?" he repeated.

She moved to the wall behind them. He looked up at the wall, organized in numbered columns of photographs. 1–100. 101–200. 201–300. And so on. She pointed him to the 600 block, where he slid his finger down the numbers until he found the picture he was looking for.

His pointer lingered for a long moment next to the picture of a woman who now obviously looked just like him, but with a red wig on, her eyes dropped, lips parted.

Red.

His other hand came to his mouth again.

Dune felt a shock wave move through her. This was impossible. The only person she'd brought home? The person whose ashes were in the yard, mixed with those of her mother and grandmother? That was *his* person?

Long minutes passed.

"I knew. I mean ... I figured." She thought that's what he said—only gravel made it out of his throat.

"I'm so sorry," she said.

As Dawud read the words next to the picture aloud, his radio voice distorted by a grainy tremble, Dune remembered Red.

"November 5th, #654 found 10:13pm in front of 1956 Outer Drive. Grocery bag tipped over at her feet, some food starting to spoil, indicating she'd been there hours."

Dune remembered Red's arm, curled at an angle from her chest, still holding the ghost of the grocery bag laying at her feet. The bag had been torn, some creatures had been at it. Her wallet was untouched.

Dune had hoped the pictures, names, recordings and details might be some comfort to family members if her data ever got shared with those surviving beyond the city. This was her first time getting to share with a stranger this work that had obsessed her for months and it was mostly an accident, a result of needing to be close to this man's voice and aliveness. What were the odds this was Red's kin? She yearned for any mathematical capacity.

Her hope was that this was going to be a comfort to Dawud and not more pain.

"Words: Juan, home, dance, kiss. AUDIO. Audio?"

Red's words had stood out to Dune because they seemed to paint a picture of a very specific memory and, more importantly, a moment that seemed happy. She experienced this sickness as grief, but Dance? Kiss? Home? Who was Juan?

Red had spoken her words with a slight lilt that made it feel like a song. A love song. A chant.

"Died November 8th? I just missed her."

As devastating as it had been to watch Kama and then Mama Vivian die, Dune had experienced their last moments. Now that felt like a balm to her system, to know they had been cared for by someone who loved them. Dune was so grateful now that she had brought Red home, alongside the familiar and yawning nausea in her gut for all the people she hadn't been able to care for.

Red had been tenacious in the realm of the sick. She'd made Dune feel hopeful for a moment.

Dawud looked at her, his eyes sharp and searching. "Audio?"

Dune nodded, moving to the far back of the basement. Next to the washer and dryer was the desk with a filing cabinet tucked under it, topped with hard drives stacked around Kama's old laptop, behind which was Brendon's antiquated PC. Dawud set his jaw and followed her over.

Sitting at the desk, Dune moved her fingers over the keys with a light touch, not looking. She pulled up a spreadsheet on the computer, found the line she needed, picked one of the hard drives marked with sharpie ink and attached a yellow wire to it. Soon the screen showed a set of folders organized by numbers. She searched and then opened 654. There were two files.

She stood up, gestured for Dawud to sit down, and handed him a set of large soft headphones.

He clicked on the first file.

She watched for a second as he listened to the recordings of 654, Red saying her four words over and over on the day Dune'd found her. Then she looked away—his face was a private one.

She opened the 400–700 cabinet to find the additional file her database told her she'd stored for 654. She pulled out a folder, flipped it open and saw three more pictures of Red from her time in the yellow house. In one picture the woman was calm, her eyes open and clear, almost normal beyond the gaunt cheeks.

She set the folder down next to Dawud and stepped back quietly, heading upstairs, leaving him there to let go.

. . . .

When Dawud climbed out of the basement an hour later, Dune

was sitting at the kitchen table smoking a small joint. He sat down next to her, avoiding her direct gaze, hitting the joint when she offered it.

"Bethany Brown. My sister."

"I should have seen it."

"Seems like you got a lot of faces to remember. She really the 654th person you found?"

"Yeah. And ... I called her Red. Red was the only person I brought back here, actually." She paused there for a moment, in the uncomfortable destiny of this truth, that the only two strangers she had invited into her home during this virus happened to be siblings. She felt a chill as he looked up at her. His eyes sparked her mercy; she'd save the story of Red's stay, he could request it when he was ready to hear it. "I documented 671, mostly right here in the Corridor, maybe a hundred or so around the city."

The quiet settled between them easily, remembering the virus in its snaky unfolding, gathering the conversation in parallel.

"Our official numbers say around 124,000 were infected, but that's people who came in, or were called in, or we found in our city sweeps. We know there are homeless people we didn't get and we are sure people took sick family members out of the city before we set up the boundary. Including all the missing people reports since last summer, we're estimating one in five Detroiters died from H-8, all of whom have African diasporic lineage." Dawud seemed relieved to shift into the business of their visit.

"I was hoping we could maybe combine our data somehow," Dune tried to match his formality. "I don't really have a way to share this stuff with people who might be looking."

Dawud took a deep inhale and closed his eyes.

"We—we're only tracking the living. Were. Our mission was

to contain the virus and to get people away from the source of H-8 to a refuge where we could watch to make sure they didn't get sick."

"These people are living." Dune gestured downward and Dawud's eyes acknowledged the breathing ghosts in the basement below. "Were."

"We would argue that they were dying." His voice was soft, but uncompromising.

Dune nibbled on the inside of her lip. "What if we could stop people from getting sick? If we just understood them?"

"Understood them?"

"Yeah. Understood why they—what makes them sick. The cause of this effect. What they're talking about."

Dawud was quiet again. Dune began to feel foolish, naive.

"Juan was Bet's baby daddy. Basically. She had two abortions by him. They'd been sober together for three years last time I saw her—that was ... maybe two years ago. He ain't like me much." Dawud swallowed a thought. "I ain't like him either for a long time. But they were finally doing aight I think. Sounded like it. She never picked up the phone when I called." He looked her way. "Juan was in my files, seems like he got sick a few weeks before she did. But she wasn't at her house—that's ... She was where we grew up. Renting that out was her income stream."

Dune felt the edges of their stories reaching each other, wanting to complete each other.

"I want to weave it all together. Like that."

"What does it matter?" He wasn't rude, just matter of fact.

Dune felt like her father, wanting to defend history for its own sake. "I think this is bigger than Detroit. Maybe we're just the first. I want to understand what it is. I'm not a scientist, I can't understand what's happening inside ... but there is something that makes H-8 take some of us and leave the rest. Why is that?"

Dawud nodded, thoughtfully.

Dune took a deep breath, feeling her spine all the way down her back. "Honestly I don't know. Was it useful to you, what I gathered about your sister?"

Dawud closed his eyes. He smiled tightly. When he opened his eyes, she realized she could see more of him somehow. "Yes."

He continued, "For the death count, we didn't track like you. And, to be honest, there's no *we* now, just me and the rotation holding down the perimeter. HQ mostly stopped talking to me.... It was 'rebellious' when I asked to stay. Now they just waiting for me to die. That's why I started the show, to try and document what it has always been like, what it feels like now, and kind of say fuck you to everyone for leaving it behind like this."

Dune felt the anger move like a wave through his body, felt it land back into a quiet place. "So what did you track?"

"The date they were found, the neighborhood. But we lacked your curiosity," Dawud chuckled a bit. "We were just trying to contain and eradicate the threat. We didn't pay attention to the specifics, the places, or what they're saying. How you even understand them?"

"Um." Dune felt Marta's presence for a second as she gathered a response. Marta could understand all kids. In any state of learning to speak, any snotty communication, she would listen to what sounded like gibberish and reply coherently. "It's like when you love a kid. The more you listen, the more you want to understand, the more you hear. Anyway, it's only a few words. Each person who's speaking is repeating one word, sometimes as many as five. And they don't all speak. But those that do? They repeat, they all repeat. Maybe it's something about the place where they get sick?"

Dawud's face showed real surprise. "Like, certain places *cause* the sickness?"

"I don't know. Not *just* the place, cause my mom and I were in the same place." Dune paused. She couldn't say it to him yet. "I think it's more about the relationship. Between the place and the person. Most of the people I find are looking at some place. Intensely. Like, it's not even that they got sick. It's like they ... realized something?"

"Realized what?"

Dune felt her face tighten, processing whether to trust him with hypotheses.

"I'm listening." He leaned toward her.

"It feels like the grievers realize they have to stop everything and ... grieve. For something. Something lost. Or everything they've lost." Dune finished and winced a bit, feeling equally certain of and embarrassed by her own conclusions.

"Grievers."

"Yeah. Did you ever see someone who just got sick?"

"I think so. Not sure, really."

"The first thing that happens is they look like they just received the most ... the worst news. Shock. Before H-8, you get shit news, that shock happens, and then you collapse and cry and be depressed. And then your life goes on. But with H-8 they never recover. They get stuck in that initial shock of grief forever. So ... yeah. I thought, grievers."

"Some asshole in my unit was calling them zombies. Grievers makes more sense. So ... you want to combine the data. You have numbers, some names, addresses where they were found, and pictures. We have missing people's names and out of state destinations."

"I want to put names and stories and conclusions to some of these faces." *And I want to not be alone*, Dune added in her mind.

Dawud rubbed his chin. "We could try. People were so scared by the time they left, it was hard to get them to answer any questions. But—I'm thinking we could do something about getting more people's stories. Survey the evacuated people."

Dune felt almost hungry at that idea. She nodded, trying to contain herself, trying to stay cool. She remembered Elouise, the sharp cut of losing her auntie almost immediately after reconnecting. "Do you ... What happened when you found grievers?"

"Depends. Families with resources, they got they people hospital beds, ventilators. Most people, we were housing them at schools."

The last time local news was being produced regularly they had been worried about reaching capacity in the weather appropriate spaces. That was before winter. "Did they fill up?"

"The schools never filled up faster than the bodies went out."

Dune's mouth moved against her wishes. "Is it true you used the incinerator?"

"I was never on the disposal or transport teams." Dawud looked uncomfortable and sounded disgusted. "I heard rumors though."

Dune had been holding onto this one, waiting to tell someone about themselves. "We don't know how it spreads. It seems really heartless and dangerous to use the incinerator."

Dawud shrugged, not the one. "Yeah. I don't know. I can try to find out. Like I said, the guard is mostly withdrawn. Not worth risking any personnel to move people who clearly don't want to be moved. But I can radio over, tomorrow. What did *you* do with the bodies?"

Dune flushed, realizing in that moment that her backyard cremation method was really no better than the incinerator, just much smaller.

"Wait." Dawud held hands up. "I'm not ready." He smiled at her, but it looked pained. "There's time."

As they sat and smoked, the weight of the high came over Dune's eyes and she felt fully comfortable for the first time since they'd met.

"How long will you stay here? In Detroit?" She didn't try to control the need in her voice. They might be the last two people in the city. She wasn't going to be able to hide herself from him. That felt suddenly and viscerally clear.

He looked at her like a boy who'd just passed a test. They were going to be working together now, here in the deep end. Maybe even friends. He was what she'd wanted to find.

"Til it's done," he answered.

She smiled then, bordering on laughter. "We crazy, huh."

He smiled, too. With a shade of grief still over his face, aging him in the kitchen light, he let out a small laugh and it grew, and it pulled a laugh out of her. And they sat there, laughing amongst the dead, feeling unbearably alive.

Section Two

Marronage

chapter nine

Growing

Most of the time the basement sat in deep darkness. The fact that it was growing made no scientific sense to Dune. It was more than growing, the model was exploding with life, seemingly faster since she'd let Dawud see it. It wasn't all over, but there were thick clusters of verdant plastic around the Ren Cen.

Dune could no longer dismiss it as mold. Her father's model, her grief project, had become fecund.

The growth near the river made sense, if she forgot it was a pinned blue scarf and not an actual source of water. But the round Lego pieces from which her father had constructed the Ren Cen were almost covered in the darkest, thickest mossy growth, and here and there within the eight-mile radius of the model were singular leaves, or clusters of green. Undeniable enclaves of dense fuzzy green covered her toy home and distinct spots across the north, Belle Isle, the edges of the city, all along the river. The city itself was rimmed with green.

Down here, in the dark, Detroit was growing into a lush jungle city.

Dune began to feel grateful that Dawud hadn't wanted to come back down after finding Bethany. Alone, she could accept that the model's growth was just nature taking its course.

....

Dune was floating on her back in the middle of the Detroit River.

The water was moving really quickly around her, but she was barely moving, able to see the Ren Cen on her left and Caesars casino in Windsor on her right. Then she noticed that the Ren Cen was turning green from the bottom up.

She flipped over in the water, treading. The green was growing all along the water, not just on the buildings. She started to swim closer, but then there was a garbage barge between her and the city, and then another, their wakes and stench pushing her back. She started swimming faster. With each stroke she felt further and further from the city, more and more desperate to reach it, water pulling her down, making her cough.

A barge cut right in front of her, spinning and tossing her in the river. When it cleared, there was a wall of green in front of her, all the way up to the clouds above, all the way up and down the river.

She was outside Detroit.

....

Dune moved around the house following small impulses, everything either taking her down into the basement or up away from it. It is the accumulation of small movements, most seemingly without purpose or direction, that make the world, that make a life.

She noticed how often she was having brief thoughts about Dawud. Where was he, what was he doing, was he lonely, was he thinking of her. These weren't romantic thoughts; they were both gay and perhaps that was for the best. These were empty cup thoughts near a faucet, near a creek.

She knew why she kept inviting him over, but didn't really understand why he came around. He was bombastic, dynamic, weird, and intriguing. She was ... quiet, focused, and sad. Quirky, sure. Mysterious, but in the way of shy people more than fascinating ones.

They'd spent the last two weeks exchanging stories, her looking at the chaotic National Guard maps of the city, him looking through her hard drives. She'd given him soups, sauces, and bags of roasted vegetables from her harvesting labor in the fall. He'd brought her a walkie talkie because he expected that cell service would be more and more unreliable until the city repopulated. In training her how to use it, he'd had her laughing so hard she struggled not to wet herself. He would rather tell a joke than a truth and she was learning to explore him within the borders of his humor. He said a lot, but was rarely direct.

The Dawud B from the radio still seemed like a person she was trying to find. She wanted to see him do the show again, watch closely when he closed his eyes and began that other way of being, of speaking. In person he was so crass, had so few social graces. He burped without apology, had to be reminded to remove his boots, often held his crotch while thinking. He was decidedly not magical, even if he was excellent company. With each instance of unchecked masculinity, Dune had offered up gratitude to the goddess of sexualities for blessing her with a clear interest in femmes.

If she hadn't found Dawud B, he might have withered away in the place to be. She couldn't tell who was luckier, who had needed a friend more. Especially a friend who didn't ask too many questions about her basement garden.

The growth on the basement model was fascinating when she gave herself permission to overthink it. She paused in her moving about and made a list of what could be causing the growth, according to science.

There was nothing on the list.

She made another list of what it could be if science wasn't a factor. Though that list had a number of items, all of them were synonyms for magic.

Dune did not identify as a magical person. Kama, Marta, Elouise—she had grown up surrounded by supernatural women, drawn to the particular, determined and diasporic nature of Black women working magic. But Dune herself had always been a passenger on their ritual journeys; she knew nothing of direct magic or witchcraft.

And yet, *some* kind of magic was undeniably unfolding in her father's basement, in her mother's house. Magic was present and growing. It must have come from her parents. But was this the magic of the paranormal or the magic of illusion?

This is what walked Dune into Kama's room, where she picked up the t-shirt that held her mother's bones, hugging them close to her. These bones had formed inside her stranger-grandmother, these bones had carried Kama through a childhood shrouded mostly in mystery for Dune. Each instance of intimacy Kama had known had reverberated through this stack of bones—these were the bones that had carried Dune until she was ready to enter the world.

She could feel how she was hugging these bones and not her mother. Only that feeling allowed her to stand up with them in her arms and leave Kama's room. Seconds later, she heard Kama clear as day, "Oh I thought you was done carrying me?"

Standing in front of the basement door, Dune let herself laugh—that specific joy that only lives inside grief—visible only through the lens of loss.

She awkwardly opened the door without dropping her precious, featherlight cargo. She brought the last of her mother's body down into the basement. She unwrapped the t-shirt.

The bones seemed so fragile now, so far from being attached to each other, carrying weight, dancing. Holding Dune. Birthing her.

Dune picked up two of the smallest bones and laid them down where Southfield crossed 8 mile. The peak of the city curved into the v of bone. Dune felt a bit of pull in her fingers and surrendered to it, picking up more bones and laying them along 8 mile, over to Telegraph, cutting across at Michigan and then down Southfield, lining the city down to the water. She placed bones along the river, on the Canada side.

The final bone she picked up was a curved rib. She placed it near Grosse Pointe, from Vernier to the water. As if it had all been measured out beforehand, her mother's rib completed the barrier on the land, enclosing the city.

"Mother," Dune whispered, placing her palm over her heart. "Protect us."

The basement was thick with silence, hundreds of ghosted eyes watching over a city held together by motherbones.

chapter ten

Mundane

Since Dawud had joined her, their work had kept her closer to the Corridor. About a month into their friendship, Dune woke up certain that it was time to check the perimeter. She wanted to go look, to test her unspeakable theory, that placing her mother's bones in the basement the week before might have had some magical impact on her living world.

She started packing while still in her boxers and t-shirt: her notebook, camera, some snack bars, hand warmers, a few bottles of water. She planned to bike the entire perimeter, about forty-five miles.

Dawud showed up to the door while she was pulling on a second layer of sweatpants. She'd hoped to be on her way before he got there, but he was early. He didn't ask for the plan, just walked back to his bike and waited patiently, propped on the seat.

"You up for forty-five miles?" she called to him.

Dawud screwed his face up at her and they both laughed. "I'll drive."

Dune sat in the passenger seat of her ancient brown Chevy Cavalier, directing Dawud to follow the Bridge to Canada signs and then cut west, down to where the Southwest neighborhood kissed the river. Her plan was to track the water all the way west to Southfield Highway, take that up to 8 Mile and then across until they hit Jefferson and wound their way home.

She appreciated Dawud's ability to be quiet. Since he had confirmed there were no more evacuation patrols circling for the Guard, she'd felt a bit more comfortable traversing the city during the day, more on guard for other survivors like herself than official jailers. But when he came with her, with his camo and his gun, she could feel herself actually relax into a feeling akin to safety. It wasn't that he was tougher—he was more scared of most things than she was. He'd been visibly upset about her months of entering houses and walking amongst the dead to bring forth supplies and stories. But he was trained to protect himself, to shoot without killing, to handle a weapon that earned more respect than her amateur knives.

She wondered what her nonviolent father would make of this.

"You know, I'm also an orphan," Dawud suddenly offered into the reflective space.

Dune glanced sideways at him, taking a moment to catch up to his use of the word "also."

"Dad overdosed while Mom was pregnant with Bets. Mom died a couple years ago, cancer." Dawud was looking intently at the steering wheel in his hands as he spoke, picking at a place where the pleather from last century was peeling. Dune kept peeking at him, he didn't sound finished. Finally he looked up at her, "When my Dad died, I was a kid. And I made a place to go and talk to him, in my closet."

Dune flushed, cringing as if Dawud had just flipped on a floodlight in her dark sacred basement tomb.

"When my Mom died, I was pissed. It felt like if I don't get a dad then I should get my mom forever, or until I'm really old at least. And cancer is such an unreasonable asshole. My mom was as healthy as a single Black mom can be—yoga mat at the end of the bed, chakras aligned, Yemeya on deck; but never enough sleep, eating in transit, secret cigarettes. And doctors who sent her home with stomach pain for a year before she asked if it could be cancer. By then it was everywhere. She said the MRI looked like it was snowing inside her."

Dawud paused, his bitterness thick on his tongue. He drummed the steering wheel.

"I'm so sorry, Dawud."

Dawud nodded. "I think H-8 is an even bigger asshole."

Dune nodded. "I think however it happens, it's shit. But it feels so much worse when you know ... you feel like it wasn't supposed to be like this."

Dawud looked at her for a moment and seemed to open a secret door in the wall between them. More of her was able to flow towards him, just looking. She could feel more of him with her. He smiled at her, squinting a bit, like she was bright.

"I write to them. Letters. Mostly to my mom, but sometimes to my dad too."

"About what?"

"Lately, about how their Detroit has changed and if they have any clues about what happened here. And about you—"

Dawud slammed on the brakes mid-sentence. Dune jerked to attention.

They'd reached Southfield, a D-list highway that was now a

bizarre, impossible landscape. On the right side of the street, the southern side which reached towards downtown, things looked pretty normal. Strip malls, auto mechanics, small businesses, and coney islands as far as the eye could see. Everything closed, dusted with snow, in the bleak black-gray of Michigan winter. Because there weren't people driving around in it, the snow hadn't devolved into the usual brown sludge. Still, it was winter, and no one would be tempted to get out of the car and walk around.

Across the highway though, it was feral. You could still see the shape of businesses that had been there; flat low buildings, golden arches, signs and awnings were visible. But there was growth everywhere, vines spreading up and over the buildings, moss along the ground. There was a tree coming out through the roof of a decrepit Coney.

Across that highway it was summer.

In twenty years.

Dawud tried to put it into words. "The fuck?" is what came out.

Dune was shocked, even if she may have had a hand in it. She didn't turn from the growth, whispering, "I was just out here last month—it looked normal!"

They pulled the car around at the first U-turn and walked up to the green border. Dune squatted down close—there were little mushrooms, bright orange caps on cream stems, under the bushes in front of her. One vine had a white flower blossoming every foot or so. And she wasn't sure, but it looked like the vines in front of her were moving, possibly growing.

Dune reached her fingers down. She wanted to touch this growth, to know it wasn't some strange hologram or mirage. She needed to know they weren't sharing a hallucination, suffering a viral evolution of H-8. As she moved her fingers towards the closest flower, it seemed, just ever so slightly, to lift towards her.

"Dune!" Dawud caught her wrist before she could make contact. "Maybe not until we know what it is … could be poisonous? Connected to H-8? Anything?" He was speaking to her slowly, as if she might not comprehend common sense.

She had to tread carefully with Dawud, her only companion in the known world. She didn't want to lie. But she couldn't share that she had either gone completely batshit or was literally growing walls around the city by manipulating her father's toys and her mother's material detritus in the basement.

Or both.

So she didn't mention the witchy model, the flourishing green that wasn't mold, the bones she had used to edge around the city borders. She didn't mention her dreams of wild, jungle-ish walls, just like these would become if they kept growing.

She wanted to trust Dawud. She just didn't know how to say these things.

An instant later there was a cacophony of sound as a mass of birds lifted from a nearby roof. Dune and Dawud stood, mouths agape, following the murmuration with their eyes, the largest formation of starlings either had ever seen. The birds expanded and contracted like blown glass, smooth and sleek. Dawud's hand softened from an intervention to a hold and they stood, holding hands, watching the birds until they couldn't see the mass anymore.

"Let's see how far this goes," Dawud said, reclaiming his hand for his pocket. They got back in the car, both in their own heads about what they were seeing.

They didn't make it all the way around the perimeter. It was too disconcerting, driving through the half-wild. Dune had found what she needed to find, she wanted some alone time to make sense of it.

When they finally turned and began making their way back to the house, Dawud had begun brainstorming options for what had caused the growth. He swore it wasn't the work of the National Guard—"we don't recruit green thumbs!" His favorite idea was that some radical racist farmers from the rest of the state were trying to overgrow the city, disappear it.

Once they got to the house, they were sore and hungry. Dune was grateful when Dawud realized she didn't have the capacity to make any further sense of what they'd seen, when his questions abruptly stopped. Her need to be alone transmuted into a need to be at ease. Without anyone saying a word, they decided to get drunk.

At least, Dune was definitely drunk and Dawud seemed to be next to her in it.

"Look. Listen." Dune was pulling together her argument. "It's a moot question. She's foundational text."

"She's definitely emotive! Like no doubt ... she sounds like she used to feel real emotions. But lyrically—like a text is made of words." Dawud was passionate, even when wrong.

"But she's foundational! Everything you can possibly feel sits between *Real Love* and *Not Gonna Cry*!" Dune toasted both ends of this spectrum and then herself.

"Not at all—neither of those songs includes actually being in love. To make your case you have to include *Sweet Thang*. Which, lyrically, is Chaka Khan. And I think it was still an affair or something."

Dune daggered him with her eyes. "You might be enjoying you right now, but I am not enjoying you right now."

"I'm not saying Mary isn't one of *your* core memories, padawan, or even like—not crucial to Black people understanding our souls. I am just saying she does it through wailing. I daresay off-key wailing, sometimes. And maybe she would be better with no words."

"Nina was off-key sometimes you know."

"Nina was an emotional genius, and a pianist who happened to sing for historical documentation. I don't think you even want to take any steps further down that particular path. I still respect you."

Dune laughed too loud. She was on the floor of the living room, leaning against the couch. Dawud was sitting in the armchair, legs crossed, the bottle of Jameson in arm's reach. They'd had three, maybe four shots each.

"You are wrong, sir. You are outdated. In this dancery. You sound old. It's embarrassing for you."

Dune leaned her head back and that was dizzying, so she sat up and squinted, trying to get her vision to solidify.

"Fucking drunk," she said, in case Dawud was missing the signs.

"Lightweight," Dawud shot and then poured himself more Jamey.

Dune lifted her glass and then set it back down. "Fuck you. Ok but do you recognize the supremacy of Mariah Carey?"

"Not even a little bit," Dawud laughed and pointed his finger at her. "Divas blow it all on the first album and then it's like they line up the songwriters and shoot em dead."

"Mariah wrote her own songs though," Dune motioned dropping a mic in the air.

"She caved to peer pressure. Intimidated peers were like, 'Eight

95

octaves? Naw, sing in a baby voice while rappers rap.'" Dog came padding in and stepped over Dune's legs to curl up at Dawud's feet.

"And yet there are hits. Baby voice diva hits. "Fantasy"? "Heart-breaker"? These are classic songs."

"Dune. No. Just because DJs play something everywhere doesn't make it a classic song. It makes it a popular song. There is so much space between popular and classic that they should each get their own planetary distinctions."

Dune shook her head. "Ok, can I just ask you one question?"

"Shoot," Dawud responded, raising his glass to her.

"Are you a hater on purpose or did it just kind of happen to you?"

Dawud spit his drink at her without apology. He missed, but she sat in shock.

"I don't think having an accurate critique makes me a hater. It just makes me smarter than you."

"Oh!" Dune actually let her jaw drop, sharpening. "No sir! Love appears to have been surgically removed from your heart and you are no longer able to be a true fan of anything good."

"I just like shit harder."

"Oh?" Dune cocked her brow, flirtatious, then caught her-self and erased her own face, going blank. She settled on a TV anchor smile, looking at the carpet. She couldn't be flirting with a dude. She couldn't imagine having to deal with a penis, not in the slightest.

"Oh. Very hard. I'm talking death metal, people screaming bloody throats and shit. I don't know why, it goes against my care bear nature."

Dune lifted a toast to that. "Care bears—prepare to stare!"

Dawud looked shocked now—"How do you know that?"

"Oh, I'll show you my belly sometime."

....

Jizo was small and often made his way through the world unseen, walking alongside of and under things, quickly disappearing when people came around that were not Captain. His job was to go into the world and forage, bringing things home for them to eat.

Captain liked things in cans, Jizo liked things that grew out of the ground. He usually brought back a mix of the two. Today he had a nice sized bundle under his left arm.

He was approaching the house when he saw two people standing near it. He spotted them before they saw him and tucked himself against the side of a neighbor's abandoned porch, lowering his body until only his eyes peeked over the top of the stair, silently placing his bundle down beneath his feet so he wouldn't drop it if startled.

The two people were laughing, talking to each other as their eyes swept opposite sides of the street. The one looking at the right side of the street was a boyish woman in a baggy, loud coat. She had a smile that crooked to one side in a way that made her whole body seem to lean. She seemed harmless.

The other one was taller, broad shouldered with a round belly stretching against his sweater. He wore the pants and jacket with woods on them and serious boots, he must be one of the hunters. They usually moved in larger packs.

As they got closer, Jizo slid all the way down against the stair and tucked himself up under the edge, pulling his black shirt over his head and arms and curling up on his side. They moved past without pausing. He couldn't hear their words, just the sweet way they sounded together, voices swooping in and out of each other like bird songs.

When their songs had faded, he unfurled his body, retrieved his package and ran home. He scurried into the house Captain had made theirs, leaving his shoes just inside the door to the stair and padding his way up into the darkness.

The door was locked from inside, but Jizo had cut out a smaller door for himself from the bottom panel. To open it he merely pressed the weight of two fingers against the right side. It popped open and he rolled into the house. He walked the bundle over to the table and spread it open. Inside of an old scarf was a small treasure trove. Two cans of southwest black beans, a can of garbanzo beans and a can of sweet peppers for Captain, two heads of dirty lettuce and a handful of radishes for Jizo.

He was excited for Captain to see what he had. He padded around the house, wondering where Captain was. Usually even when he was very quiet, Captain heard him. But today he heard no Captain.

He walked through the kitchen and into Captain's room. The old man was sitting quietly in his chair looking out his big picture window. He was rocking back and forth. Jizo ran over to him and placed both hands on Captain's wet cheeks. Captain looked over at the boy and for a moment he was totally still.

Then a sheepish grin dawned on Captain's face. "I'm sorry Jizo." His voice was very quiet and seemed to be thick, "Almost lost it there."

Jizo wiped tears off of Captain's face.

"I miss my Delilah. Sometimes it's like she standing *right* behind me. Like if I'm still. Next to me ... taking a breath on a hard day." Captain's eyes looked into the space next to Jizo and the boy knew the old man was time traveling. "She wasn't like no one else. And I wait and just feel her close as long as I can and when I look, and she isn't there ... it hurts in a brand new way sometime. Like she just left. Even though she been gone! And I know she gone."

Jizo knew that feeling.

"I wish you could have met her. Oh I wish she could have met you boy! The sweetest woman in Detroit every day that I knew her. Not sweet like you could push her over ... Sweet like how fire tastes on a rib, deep in there sweet, can't tell flesh from bone, her from me sweet. She can get me waxing, whooo! To this day. Best decision I ever made."

Jizo smiled softly. He understood. He always understood.

chapter eleven

The Shy Comet

Dune couldn't get her jeans up. She had dried them, but that usually wasn't a problem. She had had to suck it all in the past few times she got them on. Now she hopped up and down, wriggled, zig zagging, like she could convince the pants to let her in.

They didn't.

She had grown up a slender tomboy, playing basketball, soccer, jogging. Her lovers had carried the weight and she had loved taking handfuls of them, folding herself into their soft thighs and bellies.

She placed her hands now around her own belly and pressed in gently. She slid her hands down and over her thighs, her own ass. What she felt in her hands was solid with an amazingly resistant give. Fat. Her own fat. She had never felt this before.

She felt embarrassed by what was in her hands.

She was also a comfort to herself, even if it felt like touching a stranger.

Dune went to Kama's room and opened the closet. She pulled

out black leggings and a hip-length green dashiki top. The leggings let her relax, moving with her body. The dashiki was full bodied and she felt her belly loosen.

Looking in the mirror she thought how hard Kama would laugh to see her like this. That thought was tender around the edges, so she left it there, unexamined.

When he saw her, Dawud said nothing about her outfit. To reciprocate, she didn't read his t-shirt, which seemed to have someone urinating on it.

That night there was a comet passing overhead that should be visible to the naked eye. Dawud convinced her to come look. The sky was remarkably clear, rare for Detroit in winter. The comet was shy. They lingered on her stoop in the snow-bright dark, drinking foraged Jameson and sharing a spliff. The substances softened Dawud into his memory.

"You know, I worked at Honest John's for years," he nodded his chin towards the bar they could almost see around the corner. "Junkies used to turn this street into a frightening and magical runway. There was the rollers—two men in wheelchairs. One had a motorized wheelchair, the other didn't. So you'd see them go by, one driving his wheelchair and the other one holding on and getting pulled along, both of them just yapping." Dawud looked down the street like they might appear.

"Do you remember Pepe le Pew?" Through her breathcloud, Dune could see the street dancer's spot from where they sat.

"The loverman?! There was one woman, I guess probably she was working the street, she was real fly. Heels in winter and it looked ok. But she would walk by him and he would howl, from the moment she was in sight till she was out of it, he was yelling at her how she was too fine."

They laughed, remembering different eras of the neighborhood, different stars of the street. Dune savored the way the laughter moved through her body. Dawud was hilarious, but he also listened to her, her quiet wit. At first, she'd felt guilt for the amount of laughter that took place between them. It was getting easier to laugh, easier to just let the moments be between them.

He switched topics abruptly on her, catching her eyes and not looking away. "Mostly I sleep with men."

"Yeah?" Dune smiled a bit, stunned but catching up. "Mostly I sleep with women."

They each let that sink in for a minute.

"You aren't my type. Generally." He slung this low, still looking at her, putting on the air of someone being quite serious and quite frank.

"Yeah?" She made a studious face, looking him up and down. "You're my anti-type."

"You sexy, tho." The grin on his face looked like he was surprised at himself. "It's weird."

"You too. And, you're alive." They laughed, nervous energy sitting between them.

Dune had never made a first move in her life, letting the pretty girls come to her. But everything else had changed. She rolled forward off the stoop and spun on her knees until she was facing him. She placed her hands on his thighs and closed her eyes, trying to remember the last time she had touched a man with any intention. High school?

He was solid under her palms.

Dawud reached down and took her waist, pulling her up into his lips. It was an awkward kiss, wet, teeth clashing. Dune pulled back with a grimace.

"Don't handle me," she said.

After that he moved in slowly and kissed her again, his touch soft. She relaxed and the kiss was good, with the promise of great, pulling their bodies closer and closer together.

Dune was shy about her changed body. It was soft in all the places she'd prided herself on being hard, her thighs dimpling, belly folded on itself. Her hips had new marks moving up the skin like sun rays. As they kissed, part of her mind kept rushing ahead to that unveiling moment. But his body kept inviting her back, setting her at ease. He was strong and his belly was so round and solid, it felt good, she liked how it curved into his hips.

When they realized it was too cold on the porch to enjoy anything intimate, she led him to her old room and they disrupted the dust.

It didn't take long. They were bodies and they needed to be touched. The whole thing was actually very easy.

Dawud stayed.

For two days straight they fucked and slept, leaving bed only to get water and food, to rinse off between fucks. There was nothing else they needed to do.

. . . .

On the fourth day they found themselves looking at each other in the eyes on the edge of orgasms. Almost immediately Dawud was laughing. This unsettled Dune and they laughed together across the threshold, not letting go of each other. After that they began to hold each other on the way to sleep. Dawud was into cuddling and Dune enjoyed it more than she remembered.

Their desires remained queer in this configuration and they both got to stay in the dignity of their own masculinities—she dominated him, entered him, topped him; he surrendered, submitted, power bottomed. Dawud, cooking them pancakes from a box after a particularly passionate session, said, "Maybe this is the queerest sex we could have."

"How you figure?" Dune asked, not convinced, not disagreeing.

"Well my norm is men. I like tall, thick bears of men. Hairy, burly, monsters who make me feel small and irresistible. What's your type?"

"Ah. Power femme nerds. Soft women, curvy. With sharp minds and sharp nails."

"Right, so that's our norm, right? We are homonormative!"

"No, we are queer normative. Homonormative is something else, like, recreating the hetero dynamics even in gay shit."

"Ok, fair, professor. Queerish, hetero-odd. Whatever the fuck. What I'm saying though, is that for us, the more transgressive or strange behavior, would be the hetero experience."

"I'm following," Dune smirked a bit, adding chocolate chips to his batter.

"But even in this *seemingly* hetero experience, we are upholding our gay shit. I never feel like a 'man' and 'woman?' I don't think I could do that?"

Dune nodded. "Same. We feel like ..."

"A boi king and his favorite concubine?"

Dune started laughing, wanting more. "Whose who?"

Dawud continued, "A handsome queen with her gentle knight-at-arms? The head of the household and her winsome coquette? Two dicks of flesh and silicone converged in a bed and I chose the one less girthy?"

There was plenty of time for their bodies to be queer normative, or heteroqueer, or some other awkward label for their wild pursuits. It was still cold outside, intermittent winter scraps. They had food stocked up. They both wanted to play each evening, slicking the day away, pounding it away. They were well matched for an apocalypse.

When they returned to working, it happened between her kitchen and his table at the center. He slowly brought his things over without question or announcement. At night they closed the door and escaped Detroit together.

chapter twelve

All This Data

Dawud was standing up ahead of her, doing a little jig. They were crossing Jefferson, facing the big Black fist of Joe Lewis from behind. If his Black arm of stone had continued to a body, they'd be moving within his arteries and veins. Dawud's dance was all hips, arms swinging.

"You look like you're doing the Obama dance!" She pointed at him. He turned around then, still dancing, but when he saw her he gasped, stopped dancing and ran to her.

"No, no no no Dune. Come back to me!! No!" He gripped her shoulders, in crisis. Dune felt fine, it was only slowly that she realized she couldn't move anything, the outer layer of her entire life was frozen. She couldn't move her eyes to follow Dawud as he held her and slid down to the snow covered sidewalk. He was crying against her thighs and knees. She could feel the warmth of it. She could feel everything.

She wanted to tell him how happy he had made her, this brief, extra happiness in her life, unaccounted for, unexpected.

She tried to say his name, get his attention, but nothing happened. After a long time passed, she realized he hadn't moved below her and she knew he was not going to. They were the last statue erected in Detroit. No one was coming to take them home.

Dune woke up from the nightmare, shivering in the dark and pressed herself up under Dawud, almost waking him. He threw his arm over her and soon she fell asleep again, still cold.

. . . .

"Dear Moms ..."

Dune sat holding a pen over a legal pad of paper from the office, staring into space.

She didn't know what to say to Kama. She felt like anything she could share would somehow disappoint her mother:

I've been alone in the house for months.

Now I spend all my time with a soldier and a dog, and I let both of them sleep in the house.

I didn't fight for you when you died.

Dune put her pen down.

Dog slid up against her leg, appearing as he always did, out of nowhere and necessary. Dune slid to the floor to hug him and he tucked his head under her chin. He was only the second creature to truly hold her mothergrief and he'd been through these ugly collapses for months, unflinching.

When she stood up she felt empty and wanted to be numb. Dog followed her out back, watching the sky as she rolled her spliff.

....

Dawud interviewed her sometimes. He wanted her to do the radio show with him, but she laughed him off. The place he went, that trance, she didn't want to crawl inside it, dumb it down. It was too awe inspiring from the outside.

But while she was cleaning, or canning, or cooking, she would let him interview her.

"We at ... *60 Minutes*! ... want to hear a one hour reduction of the worst crisis of your life." He'd begin.

Or, "We at *Rolling Stone* want to tell your story as a survival epic of the Detroit Techno scene. You ever been in a band?"

Or, "We at the *Nation* want to tell your story as an indictment of the modern economy."

She would look up, an innocent, agreeing to the interview with caveats about her humble beginnings.

"Who caused H-8?" Was almost always his first question. Each time she gave him a different answer.

"The Canadians. They hate being south of anyone."

Or, "Grosse Pointe City Council. They liked everything about Detroit except the Black people."

Or, "Detroit Red came back for us."

"And why, why do you think this happened in Detroit?"

To this she always gave iterations of the same answer, her father's answer. "This is fertile ground, this will be a place to survive for a long time. Someone wants this place. Someone has big plans for this whole big place."

"And in your opinion, why did the great poet Dawud B survive H-8?"

"Greatness is definitely a matter of opinion over fact. His words were strange, rambling. He couldn't be narrowed down to four, or three, or one. H-8 could not get him quiet enough to take him."

"Does God hate Black people?"

"Yes. But to be fair she kind of hates humans in general, we fucked it all up."

"Are you aware that there is a Dune action figure being sold at gas stations in California?"

"The one that doubles as a lighter? Yup. Raking in the dough on that one."

"Top three post-apocalyptic menus?"

"Oh, let's see. If I was the survivor I wanted to be, it would be a bowl of bacon and scrambled cheesy eggs. But as a mere forager? Frozen pizza, Supreme. Frozen Vietnamese chicken sausage is always a hit. Bonus wisdom: Nothing truly delicious comes out of a box or a bulk bin."

"How do you think all of this will effect Detroit's chances to reach the final four?"

Dune knew the interview was coming to a close when Dawud touched on sports. "None of our players live within the 8-mile boundary, so we'll be fine, although Tobar Sidyus has been missing in action since October."

"Is that true?" Dawud asked in an off-record aside, recognizing the Tigers player.

"True. I never found him. I looked."

"That sucks. After Shamar Alton got H-8 mid-game I suspected the rest of the team would go down quickly." They paused to let the reality pass. "So what have you personally learned from the H-8 experience that you would offer as advice to other young dykes?" He often touched himself suggestively during questions like this, as if absentmindedly drawn to his penis's needs.

"If there are no gay women around, a gay man will give you the next best gayest sex of your life." If she could keep her face straight during the entire interview, she won the evening's first penetration.

She rarely made it though. But she didn't mind starting on the bottom, surrender was good foreplay.

....

Dune was in the basement again. It had been months since she had found any new people, but she didn't feel complete with her research. It was hard not having a purpose for all the data, an audience. On one hand, Dune wanted people who had lost or left someone behind to possibly find them amongst these pictures and words.

Dawud indulged her, exporting her data to a contact in Cincinnati who was still active with the National Guard. He sent the data, but didn't say that they actually looked at it or even acknowledged the message. She didn't ask. But she was unsatisfied. There was another hand, another purpose for this research, though she couldn't quite explain what it was.

The model was half wild now, the areas that had been grazed with green now featured vines and a few flowers.

She walked in circles around the model of Detroit, the flurry of death flags creating their own patterns. She let her eyes go soft, trying to see through the solid constructed world in front of her. Each of the little slips of paper represented someone she had interacted with, someone who was now dead, and this was a small percentage of the total. It was overwhelming if she actually considered that. Who had lost more people, as quickly?

The deaths were in clusters that had formed slowly, one person at a time. The green formed some sacred geometry when she stepped back, lush at the edges, the floral patterns around the gentrification zone. The flags and the growth were in some conversation with each other that she couldn't quite interpret.

And it was green everywhere now, slung through with flags along Jefferson, all the people who'd died facing the river. All the people she'd found near the ruins of Black Bottom. The cluster near the GM Hamtramck Assembly off 75, where Poletown had been bulldozed over. The dead she'd found in each location hadn't only been older people who might have remembered its heyday, but maybe they had ancestral ties to the location? There had also been clusters of people around long-abandoned schools. That made more sense to her. There was a clearer sense of home, of ownership. But she didn't quite understand; she couldn't see the pattern clearly yet.

The green spaces didn't cluster along the same patterns as the flags. The leaves and moss crusted the top of the model, as abundant as the black flags, making it look like an architectural presentation of some Gothic Central Park housing development.

Under the table there were green roots growing towards each other, gently weaving the four tables into one. She no longer thought it was possible to separate the tables, but maybe she wouldn't need to add any more flags. Maybe H-8 was done.

Dune pressed her palms against her forehead, wishing again that she could press the truth out of her little brain. She knew there was something here, some answer, something that would soothe her when it became clear.

She walked around the model again, "Come on, come on, come on! What is it. What is it? Why? Why why why ..."

She looked up at the walls again. All of these faces. For a while they had seemed a comfort to her, but now ... now they felt like pressure. Ghosts frustrated with her for not understanding their posthumous guidance. "What was it about *y'all*? Were you all chosen for some other work? Were y'all all ideating suicide like my mother? Did you go off your meds, too? Did you feel like you couldn't get anything off the ground? Were you angry? Was it the anti-Blackness? Was it slavery? What is it? Why y'all?"

And then she noticed something new.

For most of the sick people she had documented, she had tried hard to get a precise front view of these faces, for the sake of identification later. But because these grievers weren't sentient, she could never quite get them looking into the lens. The effect had been this slight off-ness, like everyone was looking at something just beyond the camera. But now, the haunting gazes all looked past her in the same exact direction. Her skin prickled as she realized that *she* was the absence in the picture, them *not* seeing her was the central content. She followed the direction that they all appeared to be looking in.

The computer.

Dune felt the urge to run, screaming, out of the basement. She closed her eyes for a moment and felt for Kama. "I'm not scared of you, Mama. I am not scared of any of you." She willed this to be true. It wasn't, quite. But she could feel a benevolence under her trembling fear. She may not be alone, but she was also not in real danger. She moved over to her computer and sat down in front of it. She risked a look back over at the wall of faces—now they all seemed to be looking away from her in their many directions.

"Funny."

The computer held all the data. She opened a blank file. She pulled over a stack of index cards that had words on them, the

words her grievers had been whispering, or in a few cases screaming, on repeat. The nonsense.

She used her fingers to create a grid on the screen, opening it
wide.

Dune gave the command to "sort," and then pressed record.
She started reading the words out loud, watching as the grid pop-
ulated, organizing and re-organizing the words into columns and
rows, creating a system of gibberish.

"daniel, spring ... vodka, tchotchke, steak ... magic, yes ... jayce,
miracle, jesus, god, jesus, praise ... jit ... spritz, macaroni ... kiss,
dance, darkness, seventeen ... wilderness, exquisite, asterisk, nebula
... genre, deluxe ... martin, ariella, mccallan, rich ... steward, daddy,
suit ... lush, thick, morning, bluebird ... shit you never ... stop,
hungarian."

The words flowed forward, connecting, disparate.

Dune spoke the words for hours and the grid mutated before
her eyes, creating a new set of clusters that she couldn't look away
from. A shape was emerging.

When she felt hungry, she switched to the laptop and carried
it upstairs with a stack of cards, eating crackers at the table while
she sorted.

She didn't hear Dawud come in. He avoided the basement,
avoided what she was doing down there. He supported it, but
couldn't breathe deep in that place with his sister's face looking at
him from the wall.

He was standing behind her at the kitchen table as she flipped
through her third stack of index cards, reading and reading. He
leaned forward until his cheek was next to hers, looking at the grid
in front of her. She leaned against him, but then stood and went
into the living room, crossing her legs to sit and work on the couch.

When she finished the stack, she paused the recording and headed to the basement for more. He touched her shoulder and she started. When she looked up at him, her eyes were slightly softened. She had heard each of these words from the mouths of living people. Now they were words that held some mystery of the dead.

"Babe. You've been at it for hours."

"I think I'm on to something."

"What is it?"

"I can't explain it yet."

Dawud nodded. "I cooked us dinner."

Dune smiled a little with her mouth, but her eyes didn't change. "I'll be done soon."

"You won't ... that's ok. I am worried about you though, babe."

Dune's eyes drifted back to the living room, her mind in the grid. There were names of people, there were places, there were moods, colors, foods. What was the common thread?

Dawud leaned forward and kissed her on the forehead. He reached into his pocket and pulled out his phone, putting on an ancient Slum Village track, "Fall In Love." He started moving, dancing head first, his body jerking in the pantomime of breakdancing that took the rhythm but not the risk. She watched him, too surprised to do anything else. Then the music was in her, Baatin's verse frantic and playful, T3 solid, J Dilla's beat was calm, grounded. Dawud moved with total freedom, but deep rigidity, like his bones were fragile. Dune answered him with a slither—undulating. Her jaw hard but everything else fluid, like her bones were a river, energy moving along her. It felt so good to dance.

When they finished, her breath was coming hard and fast and she felt alive. Dawud beamed at her, not pushing for more. She offered her lips, her attention already moved back to her work.

"stardust, Tyson, Orion ... brisket, slow, worry, porridge ... nugget, roof, Laymon, city ..."

Dune read the words of two more stacks.

She read the words until her voice felt tired, until they were blurring in front of her eyes, until she was mispronouncing things because the letters seemed to switch places. Her ass hurt, her back hurt, her shoulders hurt. More than anything else, her heart hurt. It ached, pulling forward the memories.

She finally reached a place of satisfaction. And although she didn't think it was *the* conclusion, she had definitely noticed two things: on the grid the words looked like something rippling, like waves, a circle of waves. Second, none of the words were death, or grief, or sadness, or rage ... or anything even related to those rougher places in the human experiences. The words of the grievers were words of deep connection. Things or people they had loved and had deep connection to.

It was slippery. It was something.

She was going to go find Dawud's body and wrap herself around him. But first she pulled on her hoodie and stepped into the backyard. She stepped across the crunchy snow, over to the cold firepit. She looked up at the stars, which had tripled in the absence of light.

Did the dead puncture the sky on their way out?

Did they take all the light of their lives to some point in the blackness and explode directly over their earthly home?

Did the stars sense her existence?

....

Hours later, Dune woke up with wide eyes.

Dawud had called her Babe.

She looked down at him, curled fetal away from her, the big back of someone she had needed, had gone and found, had brought home, had taken as a lover. He had called her Babe! Easily, without hesitation or complication.

In the dark, Dune smiled so hard her teeth caught moonlight. A few times she even giggled silently, both at the feeling and at how silly it was to feel such a swoon for Dawud. She curled up against his back and lay, smiling throughout her chest and jaw, until she fell back into a deep sleep.

....

"OK, a church is on fire."

"Which one?"

"First Episcopal, down near the stadiums. Must be people, right?"

"Hmm."

Dawud was looking at his phone, reporting to her from his surveillance tracker.

Dune was scanning the city in her brain. The buildings downtown were a landscape that worked like any flesh—unremarkable taken-for-granted expanses—until some damage occurred. She cheated, thinking of the model downstairs until her memory located the church's Gothic tower, which helped her remember how it rose above Fisher Freeway in this world.

"I'm gonna go look." Dawud stood up, stretching his thick chest open, arms reaching wide.

"Wait." Dune slipped off her kitchen chair and stood in front of him. "Maybe ... I wouldn't."

He scoffed dramatically and sat back down, cupping his chin in his hand, both attentive and submissive, as if there was nothing to be done. He was teasing her fear and he kept it up 'til she conceded a smile.

He laughed as he stood back up, funny in a way she had forgotten. Funny as a way to move through crisis. Funny in a way that silently acknowledged that it would be just as acceptable to curl up in the corner.

"I'm beginning to suspect that you wouldn't have me do anything, ever," Dawud said, his voice gentle. "You would have us stay here all day, every day, cataloging people who aren't here anymore. You only came out to get me because I'm so awesome. But, darling Dune, the sun is shining and there's a building on fire. What could be more compelling?"

Since they'd met, since the first day she had brought him here, Dawud had been helping her digitize her data. He'd uploaded her lists of names into the Guard's cloud and run it against the haphazard lists of missing people his team had gathered and left for him. He didn't love research, generally, but he loved the way Dune identified patterns, cared for each story. He seemed grateful she never suggested he revisit the basement. They were closing loops, it felt purposeful, if unclear. "Come with me," he offered.

He grabbed his hoodie from the back of the chair, tying it below his high round belly, which he'd informed her a few weeks ago was not fat. When she'd responded by asking if he was pregnant, he'd shouted with laughter.

Dune pulled her mind into the present, which had the texture of a longtime lovers' spat. She didn't answer him, just headed for the door. She felt a tension towards him, an annoyance that coiled up at the base of her throat.

Their way of being around each other was getting to be familiar, but he was still a stranger when they disagreed. Arguing over a risk that could take him from her made her childlike, binary. It was simple, she wanted the power to say no.

He walked behind her for half a block and then stepped up next to her.

"Dune. What's up?"

She closed her eyes without slowing down. When she opened them, she sighed.

"I don't speak that language, honey." Dawud laid his fingers against her arm, his pressure urgent through her layers of winter gear. She slowed down and faced him. "Dune, what's wrong?"

"You don't believe me!" Her voice shook a bit. "You think you can take these risks, come out here."

"Yes. I do." Baritone, bass. "And so do you!"

Dune tightened her lips as a thousand responses came rushing forth.

"I don't think it works on me." Her voice was incredibly quiet. "It's not a risk if I'm immune."

"Yeah? And how'd you figure that out?" Dawud looked genuinely curious, but she saw the slight edge in his brown eyes, the known answer. She didn't know. She didn't know anything anymore than he did.

She turned away from Dawud, crossed her arms and stomped forward.

He caught up to her and spun her fiercely back into his arms. He hugged her like a father, a grandfather, a big brother, wrapping his arms around her shoulders, cupping her head in his hands, rocking her. He held her tight against him and she felt smushed and small, like she was bursting apart. She was terrified to truly cry all of a sudden; she didn't want to scare Dawud away from this friendship, she needed him.

Yet here she was, her face a dark window in a storm. She tried to press her eyes completely into his shoulder, erase herself. The tears came as shudders from her hips, shoulders, up through her throat, released into monstrous wails.

He held her for a long time.

When she calmed enough to catch her breath he held her away from him, gripped tightly at the shoulders.

She covered her face and didn't say anything for a minute. She didn't know how to explain what she felt anyway. The bleak shadows of loneliness had been closing in on her for so long and Dawud was a strange, unexpected light. She wanted to put him in a paper balloon and float him away into the night. She wanted to bottle him into a vial on a leather string that she could slip safe against her skin.

"I found out by watching every single person I know and love walk out here, or just fucking look out here, and not come back. And me still be here. You know?"

"I know. I believe you. We've lost everything." His voice was rough in his throat again. She was learning how he moved emotion out of that deep scratchy channel. "I still have to come out here. We still have to live."

Then Dawud's face gave way to a smile she had never seen before. The gap in his teeth, the soft lift of cheek, the alertness of his face close to hers.

"But, hey. I love you too, Dune." He reached down and took her hands in his. "I won't go. I don't have to go. Not today."

They looked south, at the black smoke climbing up the sky. Then she led him back home, up the stairs. He held her and they fell into bothered sleep, no more words needed.

....

It was three days before Dune conceded to going with Dawud to look at the church. They went in the car at dusk. They came across the highway to see a Burj Khalifa of ash reaching up to the sky, blackened stone tower connected to the husk of what had been the oldest church structure in town.

Dawud got out to take pictures and get a closer look. Dune watched him for a while, feeling a tightness in her chest that she might have to get used to. She let her eyes drift. The street was split by a divider that held a mix of snow and ash. Across the street was the glass and brick face of The Hockey Puck, a touristy pub Dune had never entered. Before her eyes could drift on towards the highway, something caught her attention. In the windows of the pub, she could see the street and the dividers, but there were flowers. Pink flowers.

Dune looked away, just to assure herself she could. Looking back, there were now people in the reflection, the street was packed like game days before H-8. Except ... except everyone Dune saw in the glass was Black. They looked at ease, they looked like life was good.

The thought crossed Dune's mind for the first time: what if she had been left behind because she couldn't choose her joy over her suffering?

She slowly opened the car door, stepping out into the brick cold with the intention of getting closer to the reflection. She first clocked Dawud, climbing up on some building rubble towards a spot that was still smoking. She turned back to The Hockey Puck. The reflection in the glass looked normal, showing the gray expanse of parking lot that reached to the stadiums which had crowded downtown. No matter how she moved, how many times she blinked, she couldn't get back in the right place to see ... what? Dune shook her head and climbed into the car, lighting a spliff.

When Dawud came back to the car, she passed him the smoke and asked him enough questions about the church ruins to get them home, to keep him from noticing her frayed edges.

....

The streets were flowing with people, a march, a parade, a dance. Everyone was dancing together, stepping forward and clapping, spinning backwards with flair, then shuffling or skipping forward again. Stopping, rolling their bodies down as if melting into the pavement. Jumping up, shimmying, everyone doing their own move for a moment before meeting again on step one. It felt so good to move, all the Black people pressed up against each other, the drum vibrating up from the pavement below. The feeling of goodwill flowed from within outwards, from her heart to her fingertips, from within this crowd out to the edges of existence. This was how they cleansed themselves of the old world—spinning it off, gyrating until the distortions could not hold. There was no painful history in these bodies, they'd stomped it out through their feet.

Dancing, she noticed herself in the glass window of the pub, her motherbody free of pain and looking delightful, dark and round as she clapped. Behind her, in the glass, she saw a vehicle parked across the street, a car she knew from scraping the snow off the windshield, from sitting in it, blowing into her hands as it warmed up in the winter. She saw the driver's door open and was suddenly pulled from the rhythm, gripped with fear, turning to yell a warning. But by the time she had turned, the realm of celebration was gone, leaving just a wintry Detroit street near an old church. No dance, no car, no one.

Everything she loved was gone.

chapter thirteen

Cells Split, then Again

Captain needed more food.

He didn't say that to Jizo, and Jizo didn't need him to. The old man was having a harder than usual time standing and sitting. He lay in bed for long hours of time, waiting for Jizo to return, waiting for Jizo to leave, trying to cover his immobility with old stories.

They needed something to change if they were going to keep surviving.

Jizo had seen the other people, the people who spoke into each other's sentences, a few more times. They were kind of neighbors, though not in the sense of living nearby—just being alive in the absence of others made the living intimates. The hunter didn't seem to be hunting anything.

Jizo set out intentionally to find them. As far as he knew they had never seen him.

He was walking his circuit, slowly. He had a clear map in his head, the houses he had foraged. He did one house at a time. He and Captain survived within the spectrum of health or not health

that each household maintained. Some houses barely had any pre-
served foods. The gift was in finding a freezer from an unhealthy
household—burritos, hot pockets, pizzas, and other things that
remixed cheese, bread, meat. Captain loved that stuff.

Otherwise, Jizo's harvest was mostly beans and canned vegetables. Captain was teaching him a lot about seasoning, creating different palettes for them with the same basic beginning materials.

Jizo wasn't sure what the other people were up to. They gathered food, but it wasn't the only thing they were searching for.
They looked in rooms other than the kitchen.

This time it took three days of paying attention, and there
they were. They were standing on the corner of Cass and Seldon.
They were laughing, in a sort of conversational dance with each
other that involved small steps towards and away from each other,
sweeping hand motions.

The brown round man bent over from his belly with laughter. The woman smirked, looked away, her way of laughing. Jizo
watched them, as he had watched them before. He knew they
were good people, the best of those he'd spotted in his excur-
sions. He didn't know if there was a way to put his finger on such
a thing.

So far, each person who had cared for him since his birth took
his mother's life had been someone he chose, based in this way.
He had gazed at the nurse with the softest heart. He had moved
towards the barren woman who wanted a child. He had lived well
in this way.

Feeling.

He was watching them from two blocks north, in the shadow
of a store he didn't like because it had someone else's pointed
house trapped in the middle of it. He moved out of the shadow

and approached them, slowly. He was small, he could slip through the air. He heard them.

"So this guy, I think his name was Harold? He owned this block, this was before they gated off the park for the Standard. He was big, ok, big in the stomach. You think I've got a gut? This dude had a swinging soft kangaroo pocket full of life, ok? So he came out here everyday, with a walkman on his head. Not an ipod, not a CD player, not even an mp3 player. A walkman. With tapes. And he would stand on this corner and do aerobics, aggressive hip thrusting, dancing. And he would ..." The man was laughing at the memory, showing it with this body. "He would sing along to the walkman. Now mind you *we* couldn't hear the walkman. Only he could hear it. But he would sing his HEART out. So you would just hear this loud ass wailing and then see him over here jammin' out. And you could get some words like, oh that's Luther, that's Whitney, that's Patti. But he was steady making songs that had no dirty parts look like the soundtrack at your favorite gentleman's club, just the dirty old man drop and thrust."

Jizo knew exactly how to get home from here and wanted to take these two there sooner than later to go get Captain. The old man needed care. Jizo was armed with the rudiments of nonverbal language now—Captain had taught him about nodding and shaking his head. He would have to build a bridge between these people with all their sounds and his own silence.

Jizo was almost next to the woman before they noticed him. The man was still deep in his story. "Yeah when the Standard came, they tried to move him out, but the patrons got into having him there, so—oh SHIT! Oh man, shit little dude!" Looking at the woman, he said, "You see that?" The woman nodded. The man dropped down to a knee. "You scared me, little guy!"

Jizo let them look at him, look all around for his adults, and then look back at him. This is how adults always responded when he chose them. His job was to urgently make them care enough to want to protect him, and then get them to follow him home.

The woman's face showed a suspicious wonder. She looked at the hunter, who Jizo noted was smiling, if a bit against his will.

"Hey," she said, almost falling as she bent down to eye level.

Jizo smiled at her.

"I'm Dune. That's Dawud. What's your name?"

Jizo looked down at his feet, still smiling. Captain would tell them.

"Ok. Where do you live?"

He pointed up Second in the direction of Captain's house. Dawud was looking around, like he felt exposed.

"Do you live with anyone?"

Jizo nodded.

"Is it your mom?"

Jizo shook his head.

"Are you OK?"

Jizo made a face of concern.

"Does the person you live with need ... help?"

Jizo was quite serious and vigorous as he shook his head yes.

Dawud nodded to Dune. "Let's go."

Dune turned back to Jizo, "Have you ever been on a bicycle before?"

Jizo smiled and wagged his sleight eyebrows, making both adults laugh, amazed. They all sensed it wasn't dire, what they were heading towards. Jizo was pleased with how quickly he'd been able to invite them over.

....

For years, Dune and her neighbors kept their bikes in the abandoned barber shop two doors down from her building. It was easier than lugging the bikes up and down her porch stairs. She found it helped to have a lot of bikes, as she wasn't the greatest at patching up the wheels.

Dog was sitting there, waiting for them. The boy ran up and hugged the creature and Dune shook her head, only slightly surprised. If dogs could smile, Dog was grinning.

She opened the janky security gate and pushed through the door, walking to a bike with a wide basket on the back. She wheeled it out and propped it on its kickstand in the street. While Dawud grabbed his bike, she ran to the house to find a pillow.

Dune created a bicycle throne for a child king with a pillow off the older couch, purple and woven and soft. She mounted it as Dawud came wheeling out a slender red bike with mountain ready wheels. She was about to ask Dawud to lift the boy into the seat when she caught his young eyes contemplating the whole contraption. Soundlessly, he ran towards her and pivoted himself up into the backseat using her arm and leg. He placed a hand gently on her back once he was settled.

Dune caught Dawud's eye to make sure she hadn't imagined it.

Dawud rode next to Dune, looking to the boy for direction. Dog ran alongside them. The kid knew every single turn, expressing himself clearly with a pointing finger. He smiled when they took corners, holding onto the edges of the basket, making it a ride, wearing a face of surprise and anticipation.

The bikes were so quick. Soon they were turning onto Holcomb.

The boy touched Dune's back again when they were in front of the house. Dune felt her neck crawl, but not because of his touch. When the first "trees" had burst forth on the basement model, one had been in her yard. The other had been on this corner.

The house the boy was approaching didn't look livable—there were holes in the front walls that could be bullet wounds, gouged out windows, burn marks up from most of the burst ground floor windows, and a general sense of structural fragility.

The boy led them around to the back, where there was a rickety stair up to the living space. He ran up the stairs, feather steps. Dune and Dawud moved up the stairs, one at a time, slow with the caution of grown-up bodies in precarious circumstances. She pointed out the orange cords running up the stairs. Whoever lived here was stealing power from a neighbor. Long before H-8 had cleared the city, it had been a matter of money to get heat, power, and water outside the right-sized zones. As the quarantine and evacuation had rolled out, downtown and midtown residents had been able to demand that heat and power keep going with the idea that they'd be back soon, and didn't want to return to burst pipes and rotted refrigerators. But this house they were entering was an anomaly—nothing should make this space livable.

The boy waited patiently at the top, and then took them inside, while Dog held a protective stance at the bottom of the stairs. It was dark, some of the walls singed from the fire that had burned out the floors below. The space was neat, the few belongings in order.

They were led through to the front room, where an old man was sitting by the window, facing them. The man was long, he looked like he would be 6'5" if he stood up. His bent legs were skinny, his knees knobby in a pair of threadbare Sunday pants. His shoulders were wide; he gave the appearance of someone who had once weighed much more, had been made of muscles since retired and hung in a closet. Now, all that was left was skin, sinew, and skeleton. But it was a soft velvety Black skin, a taut sinew, a dignified skeleton. His jaw was strong and set, his eyes had a soft blue glaze to them over the brown and every line on his face was bent around emotion.

Dune felt a bolt of fear. The old man's face could have been grief stricken and he was barely moving. But then she heard chuckling, saw a slight shiver in his old body. She realized it was laughter and that he was working his dentures inside the laughter.

"So Jizo found some people for us. Good job boy! Good job! Hello there! We sure been needin' some friends."

The man held his hand out to them, not standing, explaining, "It takes a long time to get up and down these days," and introducing himself. "Everyone calls me Captain, only there's no more everyone."

Dune and Dawud walked over and took turns shaking his hand. "I'm Dune, this is Dawud. We're both from here. I lost my mom and grandma, he lost his sister. We live in the Corridor, across from the old Coronado, near Honest John's."

Captain interjected with a pointed index finger, "I know exactly the place!"

"We have been gathering information about the sick, moving them out of the elements if we find people still alive, trying to understand the patterns of H-8 ... Dawud is National Guard." Out of the corner of her eye, Dune saw Dawud shake his head a bit at this. "Or was. How'd you manage to avoid evacuation?"

"We been up here most time since things started. Jizo immune to the thing so he do the runnin' around. I wouldn't venture it was the most thorough evacuation anyhow. I watch 'em go past here, they never look up! I was right here the whole time. They wanted to just find 'em willing to go, and I can't see goin' nowhere at this point. Spent my whole life here. Might as well die here, it's close anyway. Shoot, I be dead now but for the boy. I'm convinced I only got one more time down them stairs left in this body." Captain spoke as if each line was the punchline of a fascinating story.

Dune nodded.

"I'm glad he found us."

"I'm glad y'all could see him! Sometimes I think I made him up!"

They all looked at Jizo, who was watching them intently. Dune asked, "Do you know of any other people still alive out there?"

Jizo nodded slightly, but Captain shook his head. There was a smile that never left his old face, though it sharpened or softened depending on what he was sharing. "At first, there was a lot of people standin' out there. And then a lot of people drivin' round, sirens, ambulances, things like that. Then it was real quiet. Cold months, I been bundling Jizo up to be the only little man alive in Detroit."

"Jizo?" They all looked at the boy again.

Dawud spoke, "Nice name."

"It's a god of children, kind of a shepherd of children. Lost children. He found me 'fore all this shit stirred up and he ain't left me since, save to take care of me. For real, I think Delilah sent him, my wife. She passed on, then right when I was losing my sense of how to keep going, he shows up."

Dune, surprised, blinked back small tears. She'd been sure the kid was Captain's grandchild, but the truth, that this pair was chosen family, rocked her heart.

"Over the last few months I have documented a lot of people. We seem to be immune. Jizo probably is too. Have you left this house since the syndrome started?"

Captain shook his head. "I have not. But I don't think this thing is communible. Jizo been out there and I watched people get sick just in the middle of the street. And the timing of things. I'm not a science type man, but I can see."

Dune looked at Dawud. As far as Dune knew, these two people were the only other humans alive in the city. Dune's face took on the look of someone finding a lost and perfect puppy.

Dawud pulled up a chair next to Captain. "You from here?"

"Sholl is. Third generation Detroiter, second generation auto creator." He held up two massive rough hands. "These were the fastest in the business. No one wanted to be down the line from me, they was sure to get backed up. Hehe. Couldn't help it though. I'm a system thinking man. I can always see the quickest way to do a thing and my hands always willing, my back always able."

Captain paused, adjusting his teeth in his mouth and pinning each of them with his eyes, making sure they were listening.

"Fell in love with my woman here. Her people came up from the Carolinas and they was real proper people. Not ecstatic when they most beautiful child in the universe fell in love with a irresistible factory man, boy. But that was a good life, hehe, Detroit was a good life."

Captain turned back to the window, cloudy eyes moving over the street.

"This last period has been nothin' but Black brutality. I don't know if it could have happened to a white city. Maybe a white town. But a major city, abandoned this way? I'm talking before the plague? Nawl. I don't believe so. But I always had folks to take care of me, as long as I stayed on my hustle and as you might sense even now, I'm a stand-up guy. Not a Richard Pryor," this earned a full smile from Dawud. "Not a saint, just a good man. Delilah thought so and that got us through life. It only needs to be one person who believe in you, as long as their belief is absolute."

Captain adjusted himself between his shoulder blades, moving his neck like a lizard.

"What was Delilah like?" Dawud asked. He was leaning forward, hands on his knees. He looked like he could listen to Captain all day. Jizo was sitting on the floor now and he moved closer to Captain.

"She was ... she was really a perfect woman. An upgrade to my life in every sense of the word. She was fine as a woman can get—thick so that when you touched her she gave and she felt real. She love to be pleased, made it so I would come home and want to just please her one way or the other 'til I had to leave again." Captain sparkled and smiled speaking of Delilah, such that his love filled the room. "She had her own mind about things. She liked her own mind. That woman was completely interested in and satisfied by her own mind. If I was ever busy, sometimes when I weren't, I know she just fill herself up with curiosities of her own creation. That there was a brilliant woman. Had a healing way about her, she caught babies for everyone we knew. Her touch had a little extra warmth, she gave us all tingles sometimes just to be near her. She never watch the news, but she always knew what was what, what was happening and why it mattered. She made people feel more themselves when they came around her and then a little better about that. And she smell good. Seemed like the motherland was emanating from her pores, but with that Chanel Nº 5 on there too. She was a perfect woman."

Dune wanted to cover Jizo's ears just from the sensual tone in Captain's voice. Dawud was just smiling.

"That was just my one woman of my life. No one that came before hold a place in my memory and no one that came after hold a place in my attention."

They all sat quietly for a little while. It felt as if Delilah had walked into the room as Captain spoke and Dune knew with no question, ghost or no, that Delilah was a woman who left a mark.

Dawud started to explain where they had been, how they had met.

"I think I was starting to give up on the city when Dune walked in. Her research is fantastic. And she feels like I do—why would we leave the city now? Where would we go? What we loved was here, is here in some other energetic form. My radio show was a way of saying to myself, 'don't give up, don't give up.'"

"You on the radio! Well I'll be! Shoot. Still here, huh. You believe that young man?"

Dawud laughed. "Sometimes you yell out the loudest when you most *need* to believe, not when you have the most faith."

They all nodded together, even Jizo.

As they kept talking, Dune and Dawud were cautious about exposing their own intimate connection. This was the first person they had met who made them consider how they were perceived.

Was Captain homophobic at all? What would he assume?

They didn't present themselves as a couple, but soon Captain was fishing for information. "You lucky, boy, you know that? What if she was seventy?" And "So y'all gonna repopulate the Motor City, huh?"

Together they ignored it, quick eyes and uneasy laughter. They both liked Captain and it seemed this elder might have a lot to teach them. For instance, when he ran out of energy, he simply said so. "Okay that's enough for me. Y'all come back tomorrow."

Dune and Dawud left after this first meeting of Captain and Jizo and were quiet for a long time.

"Folie à deux?" Dawud asked as they pulled up to the house.

"No abla francais," Dune responded, lining up next to the curb. Her bike was a bit tall for her.

"Are they real?"

"Where is Jizo from you think? He's ... he's strange." Dune kept replaying in her mind the way the boy had hopped up behind her on the bike, an advanced calculation, flawless execution.

"Homeless people find each other."

"Yeah, but ... before they met?"

"He didn't say one word. But he follows everything."

"He's amazing."

"They both are," Dawud said, while Dune unlocked the back door, speaking with his hands as they pulled off their shoes. "Captain is classy. Normally all my alarm bells would be going off like 'kidnapped child' or something. But he like ... reminds me of my grandfather. He loved my grams like that. She acted like he just drove her crazy. That was my whole life. Him speaking poems to her and her being like, 'Why is my lawn overgrown then, you love me so much?'" Dawud laughed. "My mom learned from that. She treated men like shit. But to be fair, they weren't my grandfather. They tried to break her and when they inevitably failed, they got lost."

Dune filled the teapot with water and set it over the heat.

"What about you?" Dawud asked.

"My mom's parents were both auto workers, Chrysler. They did a lot of New Afrikan community work. They disowned her when she married my dad. I didn't have a way to even tell them when she died. She stayed in touch with my great-grandparents on her dad's side for a while, but they died when I was really young so I don't remember them. He got lung cancer, and mom said that on the day they learned there was nothing else to do, and that her grandfather would die, her grandmother found a lump in her breast, but didn't tell anyone till she was past the point of saving."

Dawud sat at the table, waiting for more.

"Mama Vivian, she's the one who lived here with us ... she was less romantic. Her marriages were more—sturdy. Partnerships. She outlived them both. When my Dad died ... I think my Dad was the love and purpose of her life. And my mom was the love of his." Dune felt the absence of all three of them.

"I think Captain is really lucky that Jizo showed up, wherever he came from."

chapter fourteen

Unmother

Hi Mom, hi Dad.

I found some people. This whole time alone I felt like y'all were watching me, yelling at me, "community is the answer" like you used to do every time I complained about school. Or anything. So I have a soldier friend who is also a poet and this old man who has an incredibly detailed memory. And this kid who might be a mind reader? It's who's here.

Anyway, I miss you so much. I am sorry. I am sorry for being so angry with both of you for dying. Part of me needs to blame you for leaving me. I can't figure out why you aren't here. Mom ... I can't figure out why you left me here. I don't understand, but I am trying to be curious I'm trying to make it mean something.

I am sorry for not using our time together better. You are both with me all the time these days. I'm not "going gentle into that good night," Mom. And Dad, thanks for whatever makes the basement work?

Love

Dune

. . . .

Dune and Dawud stepped out on the porch for Dawud to have a smoke. Down the street, brighter than the moon, was the Motor-City Casino, rainbow lights flashing in patterns up and down its face.

"Neon is forever!" Dawud sang, banging his palms against the porch ledge, hearkening a Jay-Z hook.

"Neon is a girl's best friend," Dune offered without thinking, a throaty modern Moulin Rouge singer.

Dawud nodded, his eyebrows lifting, his eyes flashing. He smiled, alive, and then reached forward to grab a porch beam, pulling himself up and spinning halfway around it before striking a pose.

"Sometimes you're really gay," Dune said, sinking into a folding chair, happy to look away from the lit up ghost town at Dawud's entertainment.

"Someone has to be in this family." Dawud kept spinning around the pole, turning, switching hands, bending occasionally. He was quite elegant.

"Whatchu mean?" Dune feigned defense.

"I mean ... you kind of got dicked down in this whole apocalypse." Dawud swung around so his crotch was near her face. He was smiling and she realized he was a little erect. She felt annoyed.

"Oh, like you not dick whipped?" Dune shot back. Dawud snapped to attention and dropped down on his knees, burying his face between her thighs.

"Absolutely!" He pulled her thighs tight around his head and, once again, she was laughing helplessly.

"Dawud!" Laughing. And then, pulling his head up to her, whispering, "Dawud," in a voice that made him look up at her face. She tilted his head back and thrust her tongue into his smoky mouth.

....

Dune is sitting in a chair that keeps changing shape. She grabs the arms and they are wooden and then soft woven textile under her hands. She wants to get up, but someone is standing in front of her, pulling her against a massive soft bosom. She is with her mother. She reaches around to hold on. The body keeps shifting.

"Listen for your Mothername."

"What? My what?"

"It may not be a word, it may not be a word. It's the way you will mother, the quality you have with children, they run towards you or away, they feel comfort or distress. It may not be a word. It may sound like your Mothertongue."

Dune was trying to pull back enough to see her mother's face but she couldn't. She couldn't remember what to call her mother, the softness was everywhere.

"Your Mothertongue, the nonsense you use to let your little one know they can do no wrong. You can do no wrong. Still, and forever. I'm so in love. Small and perfect. Lilolilo whoosh whoosh whoosh. Sleep now, now sleep. Sleep little boops."

Dune knew this song like she knew her mother's name and face, all of it beyond her now. She stopped pulling away and tried to dive in deeper, reaching around her mother, straining to hold on to her, wanting more more more.

Dune was struggling with the sheet when she woke up, kicking it. Dawud placed a sleepy hand on her back, not quite waking. Dune couldn't recall anything except the total presence of Kama and she felt the full-body ache of missing her mother. The tears came hard, contorting her face, reducing her breath to small shallow hitches and a few keening moans.

Dawud gathered her in, comforting her in his sleep.

....

The next day, Dune drove back to Captain's house to drop off a bag of food. She visited briefly, until Captain fell asleep mid-conversation. Jizo patted Captain's hand and brought a blanket over to put on his lap.

Dune watched Jizo move around the room.

"Where did you come from, little one?" She asked quietly, not expecting anything.

Jizo looked at her very directly and pointed up and out the window, at the sky.

"Oh?" Dune smiled, sure the boy was teasing her. "And how did you get here?"

Jizo's face was serious as he climbed up on the chair in the kitchen and then pantomimed a dramatic fall, rolling across the floor and jumping up with a look of surprise on his face. Dune swallowed her doubt.

"And why don't you talk?"

Jizo got a thoughtful look on his face and touched his own throat. He opened his mouth as if he would speak, moving his lips. Nothing came out. "You're mute?"

Jizo smiled, nodding.

Dune knew the child was more advanced than any child she had ever met, ever seen. She didn't believe in angels, but he had all the qualities she would expect from an angel.

"Do you think maybe you'd want to come live by us, Jizo, you and Captain?"

Jizo stood up from the floor, face bright as if he was receiving a present. If he'd had a tail it would be wagging. He ran a small circle, applauding.

"Ok. Ok I'll see what I can do."

Jizo ran over and clambered up onto her lap. She received him awkwardly, his limbs long. He cuddled in against her chest, under her chin. She relaxed, pressing her face against his hair.

He smelled like shampoo, honey.

He smelled like heaven.

....

The next evening, Dawud gently suggested moving the big table from the kitchen into the living room, where it wouldn't dominate the space so completely. Dune was surprised at the suggestion, at the presence of other eyes to shape her home.

She helped him move it, flipping it sideways and moving in increments. It took two hours and at times it seemed they would be thwarted by the geometry of the house, the possible angles between the narrow hallway and the doors, their different ideas of how to pull off the mission. Once the table was in, Dune had a feeling of completion, like the table would never move again. Now the library doubled as a spacious dining room and work space, and the kitchen could breathe. Dune had many ways of remembering Kama. Being severely inconvenienced in the kitchen no longer had to be one of them.

After the effort, they sprawled in the living room, reading.

The last book Kama had been reading, left open and face down on her bedside table, was *Slavery's Exiles*, by Silviana Diouf. Kama had gathered a whole bookshelf of texts about utopias and intentional communities, ranging from science fiction to highly academic studies. *Slavery's Exiles* was one of several books on the maroon colonies, though most were about international maroon communities. Diouf focused on the US South.

Dune had been following the breadcrumbs of her mother's curiosity as it invoked her own—not just utopias, but Black utopias. Not escaping to a far off land, but eking out a life hidden within the realm of previous oppression. She loved the wildness of the maroons, the ways the definitions of "maroon" traced back to the French *marron*, the Spanish *cimarron*. In each language and iteration, this word assigned to humans meant "freedom," running away from inhumane conditions, being a beast that cannot be tamed. "Being under no form of direct control from outsiders," as Diouf put it. Dune resonated with these maroons, thinking of her own life—of Dawud, Captain and Jizo, and the others who had slipped under the radar and were finding a way to live from grocery store and home raids and foraging abandoned gardens— avoiding this wave of Black death, which was far from the first and certainly not the last.

Dune also briefly thought of the street she had seen in that window, those Black faces in the Detroit sun. That unbothered look. Was she hallucinating? Was she seeing a future or a past? Was that some sort of maroon community?

Her mother had books on maroons across the Americas, including the legacy of Jamaican maroons who had run into the hills and become a part of them. Dune was grateful her wilderness had shelter, was a landscape she was familiar with already. She read how runaway enslaved people had formed a swamp community with Indigenous people trying to persist on their land. Dune wondered how the Anishinaabeg community, the Indigenous peoples of the upper Midwest still active in Detroit, were doing. Had they evacuated? Were they still here? She wondered how many people had to come together for it to qualify as a maroon space. And did it count when the enemy was not a human hunter, but a virus?

Even with all the questions, this act of marronage resonated with Dune more than any other possible description of what she and her small crew were doing. They weren't squatting, they were finding the small liberation possible beyond any white gaze. As long as they stayed here, they were opting out of the world that white supremacy had created for its own unbridled success. If they could brave the dangerous realm of the abandoned city and its viruses, maybe they could stay free.

Her theory felt too fragile to float it past Dawud yet, even when he asked her why she was reading about enslaved people's survival strategies. She couldn't piece it into a sentence yet and she couldn't tell him about the people in the window.

To clear her head, Dune set down *Slavery's Exiles* and pulled out *The Tibetan Yogas of Dream and Sleep* by Tenzin Wangyal Rinpoche. She feigned a nonchalant, almost tolerant energy as she picked it up. She hadn't told Dawud how her dreams had been feeling, how she woke up feeling like she had spent her dream hours with her mother. She wanted to see if she could find a way to be present in those visitations, to remember them, but she didn't want to tell Dawud about the places where her sanity felt like a loose tooth.

It was probably just grief. But it couldn't hurt to read.

While Dawud was brushing his teeth an hour later, Dune whispered an invitation, "Mother, visit with me tonight."

Dune waited a moment and felt nothing happen. She shrugged, and in the next breath opened her legs to Dawud, demanding a quick orgasm on his fresh tongue to help her sleep.

He briefly protested, effecting his lazy femme pose, but she shut that down with an eyebrow raise. They fell asleep quickly after, his cheek on her thigh.

· ·

The women sat at the massive kitchen table, which was now on a cloud surrounded by other clouds all kissed by a sun they couldn't see. Kama faced Elouise.

"We not ready to belong with them." Kama spit the words out, disgusted. "They didn't apologize right. Until they do, we will point and we will laugh, and we will tell them they're corny, can't dance, don't know how to wash, smell funny, and they greedy."

Elouise laughed, but reluctantly. "Now Kama ... we right a lot of the time. But it's easy to laugh at shit that's other than you. People tried to bring that when you got with B. That derision doesn't hold up. Not in intimate space. Not in sacred space."

"This how I know I'm not dead. I'm not at peace!" Kama threw her chin away from Elouise, as if her word was final.

"You think the ancestors are at peace?" Elouise smiled with her lips pursed, curving down. "But they still having our backs in the battle? How?"

"Peace comes from knowing we right on time. The battle is the next step."

"Naw, I think peace comes from being at peace. Setting down the master's tool of trynna dominate everything. Recognizing none of those boxes can hold you." Elouise's big hands were open and stretched out wide.

"How can you be at peace like that when we still dyin' in those boxes though? When we still held in them?" Kama looked hurt behind her own question.

"We love to uplift James, Malcolm, Audre, yes. But we don't always want to contend with how they outgrew the limited idea of Blackness available in their time. Each of them came to the precipice of the idea of Blackness as it was envisioned by white people and realized it was not a true container, that race as a marker of anything beyond melanin is not real. The rest is cultural and everyone makes culture. Making culture together is a path towards belonging. Those writers still belong to us, because we share a Black lineage within the vast realm of all lived experience, within the specific arc of human experience. What opened up here is a path towards belonging to ourselves. For however long. It's not perfect. But there is peace. It's not fancy. But there is enough."

Kama nodded, letting this land in her. "But how does that help my baby?"

"She gonna have to contend with anyone ready to be free. The Black people she findin', sure. And the white people ready to free themselves from the bondage of supremacy their ancestors caught them up in. And everyone else. Not in between Black and white, but all the distinct other peoples out there. That's heavy work. But it's only one planet, even if there's two Detroits on it. So she gotta deal with whoever else is on it."

chapter fifteen

Dune and Jizo

Dune came to with Dawud at her breast. She loved when he woke her up like this, slowly suckling her nipple until the sensation that actually brought her into consciousness was the tightening pressure between her thighs. He lay sideways, utterly relaxed, his soft lips pulling at her erection as she lay facing him. She watched him for a little bit.

"I know you're awake," he mumbled against her ample breast flesh.

"You're good at sucking."

He chuckled. "Lots of practice. There could be a really lovely relationship between gay men and breasts. They really are wonderful."

"I feel the same way about penises. I used to think they were so ridiculous."

Dawud let her breast fall from his mouth. "And?"

"They aight. It's what dildos are made of!"

Dawud laughed again, deeper. He scooted down the bed and pressed her legs open. Dune felt shy.

"You're hard." Dawud whispered, moving his mouth precisely against her until she tried to escape. "Stroke the shaft, worship the corpus spongiosum. Kiss and bless the glans."

When he could no longer talk, her sounds filled the room.

When she thought she might come apart, he slid one of his thick, rough fingers quickly inside her, all the way in. She vibrated in tremors around him and then contracted until his finger was pressed out, glistening.

He lay on his back across the bottom of the bed, drifting the finger to his mouth and sucking it. Dune dipped two fingers into herself and then sat forward, pressing them into Dawud's mouth around his own. He sucked all three fingers furiously and she watched him harden against his boxers with the effort. Keeping her fingers plunged deep into his mouth, she straddled him and slid herself down onto his erection.

Dawud had taken them to the crisis center and run STD tests on them both, and then researched birth control options, since she'd never used it. She was grateful for the pill he'd found; her periods were nominal and the sex was better with nothing between them. Dawud pulled his finger from his mouth and put both his hands behind his back, letting her work him. Her tightness helped a lot. Her boyish hips under her pliant belly helped a lot.

She pulled her fingers from his mouth and spun herself around on him, one somewhat awkward limb at a time. She was facing his feet, fucking him. Then she leaned back towards him until he knew he could take her the way he needed.

He crunched forward and hooked an arm across her shoulders and chest, rolling them over so that he was now on top of her, entering from behind. His face found the crook of her neck and they were breathing together as his body attuned to the feeling of ass beneath his weight. She reached up as if to scratch her neck and instead slid her fingers back into his open mouth and he began sucking again. She pressed her hips up, taking more and more of him.

They knew each others' orgasmic sensations. There was an immense tenderness in their intimacy. He sucked at her fingers and let himself move faster as his body filled with frenzy.

In the instance she felt his small warmth inside her, he was laughing, uproariously.

The first few times they'd made love she hadn't known what to do with this full-bodied laughter. It was incredible and seemed to truly come up from the root system between them—she had never experienced someone orgasm in laughter. It exploded from him and she felt him gasping, laughing with his whole body.

When the laughter eased away, he slowly rolled himself out of her. She lay there, feeling so incredibly grateful for his weight, his heartbeat, his breathlessness, his belly, his sensual guffaw. He was so beautifully alive, he was so generous with his light.

He felt her attention and turned to look at her. They lay there across the bed for some time, letting breath come back into them, becoming two bodies again, vulnerable and quiet, letting their eyes linger.

"I am so glad it's you, here, at the end of the world with me." Dawud's voice was soft, clear. "I wouldn't have picked you out of a line up of apocalypse companions. And you are just the best. The very best."

Dune felt the smile moving out from some place more central and dark than her heart.

"Shit's been so hard." She paused, feeling momentarily dazed by how little this world had to do with yesterday. "I wouldn't have wished this. But you're supposed to be here. With me. This feels right."

He reached over and graced her cheek with his thumb. Gentleness was an antidote to devastation. Gentleness, magic, and joy.

....

The backyard was snowed in, a light late-season surprise.

The firepit, still thick with ashes, was a set of suggestive lumps in the white yard. Dune didn't go out there very often; it was a graveyard to her. It was where she had said a final farewell to her family, to Red; people she'd loved, a total stranger; people she had changed liked children, people she had watched waste away.

It was a shock to her when she was washing dishes one morning and looked out to see Jizo climbing on a pile of rubbish on the edge of the yard, wood that she had gathered for fires she hadn't needed to burn. Alone and playful, he was smiling.

She rushed to the back door and opened it, calling his name. He looked up at her impishly and then down at his hands. She followed his eyes.

His hands and clothes were covered in ash and snow. She stepped out the door. He was smiling still, slightly, standing very still. Behind him, the empty windows of other buildings looked down. She felt, again, the shadow sense of otherworldly neighbors.

Jizo climbed down his conquered hill to come stand next to her. He took her hand in his, ash smudging between them. They were the same, in crucial ways that were solid outside the realm of years lived. They were the caretakers of the sick, old, dying, and dead, unafraid of the materials of death.

She felt gratitude for this small creature, amazement that he had found Captain, that without words he had kept the old man alive. How many others had he cared for? How had he learned to love in this pragmatic, selfless way? She knew he wasn't quite human, wasn't only human. She wondered again if he was an angel. Were bodhisattvas born?

She looked down at his small face and he was gazing at the yard, his face unreadable. Then he turned and looked at her. He reached up both of his hands and she reached down and picked him up. He was unwieldy to hold, but light too, light enough to shift against her hip. She felt his small breath on her collarbone.

She hummed her song for him, leaving the words at the back of her throat. "I am the basket, I am the case ... I am the only one left in this place." He was quiet, she rocked him in her arms and felt humbled by his life, his presence, his little work.

When she finished humming, he sat up in her arms and smiled at her, and then shifted so she put him down. He took her hand and pulled her towards the house. Inside, he stood by the refrigerator and looked at her expectantly. She was delighted to find that she was able to communicate with him with her eyes, eyebrows, pursed lips, smiles, holding up different items of food and drink to see what he wanted.

She would need to do something with the ashes at some point. She wasn't sure what. Should they be buried? Planted around the city like seeds? Thrown into the river?

She didn't know yet. But she would.

Perhaps Jizo would help her.

After he'd eaten two bowls of soup, she had an idea.

"Jizo, come here."

Dune crossed over to the door from the front room into the kitchen, grabbing a pencil from the counter. There were a hundred lines to track the growth of Dune when she was a child. Jizo floated over, his bare feet padding the hardwood quietly. He lined himself up with the door, where Dune made a small mark on the frame along the top of his head. He was as tall as she had been at five-years-old.

"Do you know how old you are?"

Jizo made a face of skepticism.

"This way we can watch you grow," she explained. Jizo looked very focused, almost wrinkling his brow.

....

Dune dreamt of the lush city. The living wall stretched from the dirt all the way up to the sky in every direction. The sun passed over above them, pouring down into their world, eight miles in a half circumference from the river.

The wall was green, thick, dense as a briarpatch on the horizon. Sun poured through, marbling the earth.

Dune touched it with her hands, feeling life, feeling stories in the wall.

At Dune's touch the wall reached back, wrapping vines around her wrists and pulling her in, lifting her out of gravity, moving her from vine to vine so securely that she couldn't be scared as she moved up and up and around. The living city spun her in circles around itself.

....

Two days later Jizo knocked on the door. Dune was happy to see him, she'd been planning to bring them more food that afternoon. He took her hand and led her to the kitchen, pointing at the door frame.

"Oh, yes, like next year we'll measure you again. We always did it on my birthday," Dune almost went into memory, but Jizo touched her arm and walked over to the frame.

She stood up and walked over to indulge him. He arranged himself in front of the mark she'd made two days before, facing it. Now the little J line was level with his eyes.

Dune checked him for tricks. His feet were bare, he was standing flat, not even stretching. She told him to stay, grabbed the nearest pen and made a mark, then put dates by the two marks.

Then she kneeled down and looked at Jizo in the face. She thought all her questions at him: *What are you? How are you? How can we care for you?* She also thought: *Slow down. Let the growth come naturally.*

Jizo looked back intensely, turning it into a staring contest. Peals of laughter emerged as he tried to hold her eyes. He lost in delight, hugging her thigh.

He always answered in his own way.

. . . .

Dawud looked nauseous, holding his projector cube loose in his hand like a putrid and poisonous egg. He was shaking his head, pacing, and looking at Dune, who was still breathless from the bike ride over.

"Dawud, what *is* it?"

He had walkie'd over to her to come to him urgently, that he couldn't tell her why. She'd flown. But now she wished she hadn't. He set the cube on the holster and immediately the light came on, projecting a 3-D hologram of a brown-skinned, hawk-faced man in uniform.

"My boss ..." Dawud uttered, gruff. Dune realized through

her anxiety how comforting his voice was. "Cube encrypted communique."

Dawud tapped the left side of the cube a few times until she could hear the man speaking.

"This is the most secure way I can get you this information, Sergeant Brown, and if I could make this thing self-destruct after telling you, I would." The Colonel spoke in a determined drawl, his eyes squinting as if the entire world were too bright to look at directly. "We have confirmed that as of 10am this morning eastern standard time, there have been seventeen suicides of post-quarantine Detroit refugees. These deaths started last Thursday. It is exactly seven months from the day Kama Chin was admitted to the hospital."

Dune was confused and Dawud's face revealed no clarity.

"All of the suicides have been ... white. White people who were in Detroit in the period we know that H-8 was spreading. For those who gave some indication of what, er, caused this sudden decision, we have multiple reports that they seemed to be overcome with horrific memories, falling to their knees or grabbing on to people around them, saying some variation of 'What have we done?' Some gave specifics like, 'We tortured them, we killed them. We kidnapped their children. We sold them,' before taking their lives in whatever was the most immediate way possible.

"This news has not been made public yet, but we are sure someone will put the pieces together in this next week or so and there will be panic. Unfortunately, we have something potentially much more dangerous unfolding.

"Homeland Security alerted us that a post was made on a white nationalist website that claims to be the recipe for H-8. It was taken down within an hour of being posted and we have yet to ascertain whether the recipe results in something that actually has the same results as H-8, but if it does ... Well, it's a shitshow, son. Those dumb bastards think it will just clear cities of Black people. They said, and I quote, 'Let's reclaim America.'

"We are telling you because you are one of the only soldiers with feet on ground zero and whatever this mess is, it isn't done yet. We are assessing if there is an expected threat to Detroit and, if so, we may redeploy. We need you to send us a report on whether, in your opinion, it would be safe to do so. By Friday."

Dune's knees wobbled and she dropped into a squat. The idea of H-8 being man-made had never resonated with her, she just couldn't reason it out. The idea of H-8 as a white nationalist weapon was shocking and enraging.

"Kama was killed?" She choked on these words.

"We don't know, babe. We don't know. I don't want to believe that Bet was killed, either. It could just be some dumb shit." Dawud looked just as angry as she felt.

"I've gotta call Dr. Rogers."

"Remind me who that is?"

"She was the doctor who treated my mom. She stayed in Detroit as long as she could, I think from guilt. I gave her some of Kama's bones to analyze. She had a theory that H-8 was man-made, or at least urged along by human behavior or choices."

"Dune, you can't tell her this, it's confidential."

"I know. I know! But I can ask her what she's learned."

Dawud looked at her with naked admiration. "I really appreciate your mind, Dune. Steady weaving."

Dune could feel her mind running in every direction at once, her face hot, hands tingling. Her breath was too shallow. "Is this the end of the world, Dawud?"

He shook his head, unconvincing. "Too slow."

He dropped down to one knee next to her and rubbed her back in calm, downward strokes. After some time he hugged her, awkward and tight, and she realized they were both quietly crying.

Section 3

We Aren't Alone

chapter sixteen

Others

"It is just us in here, my dear, maybe for a year, maybe for a million years, but never fear. I'm your peer and we will make a new world full of post-apocalyptic wonders, spread open thighs and arched backs asunder. Mama give me that thunder! I smell the good ocean and I am going under. The thing no one tells you is that bad company can make eternity your own private hell and good company can make the demons disarm themselves. If you can hear us today broadcasting from the Everything Awesome Circus then it is my duty to tell you about the naughty nasty pleasure dome formerly known as the dirty D. The grievers are getting it in my friends! That is right, the freaks come at night! And no I didn't forget a word, ya heard?"

Dune sat next to Dawud today as he broadcast, at her insistence. She looked at him with horror as he spoke of their sex, but he was in a trance state, his eyes fluttering, head falling back. He pointed at his head and his crotch at the same time, then switched the fingers a couple of times and wagged his hands.

Now that they had found Captain and Jizo, Dune felt satisfaction. Dawud, however, felt a different energy around being survivors in the city.

"Surely we aren't alone," he'd said to her the night before. "Surely in the rush of evacuations and the lack of resources and the plethora of stories of people who straight up refused to leave, there must be others, little bands of badass survivors."

If there were others out there, he said, they needed to know.

Dune argued, saying that she had surveyed so many places, that they couldn't check every single house.

She had written down areas where she remembered green growing on the model, "patterns." If he had noticed her recent avoidance of the basement, he didn't mention it.

Dawud made a plan to broadcast once a week, offering a meeting place. He was setting up loops that would keep the broadcast going as long as the power didn't blip.

"This might be the 153rd day of shit hitting the fan and I must declare, in here and out there, that it's finally starting to smell like roses again in every direction. Bright red, wild and romantic roses strike curious poses along the side of this very building, thorns up and out. And that is how you and me have to be if we want to be free in this great plague cage upsouth. The Everything Awesome Circus is in your hood, coming to a radio wave near you, two people plus two people make four happy people and each one of us has our own small and special magic and that means that every single thing is both good and as it should be. Come through our doors if you want some miracle cures for the righteous blues that ail you—I hail you stranger! If you hear this red rover come over, come over!

"I know you are weary of a coherent world that makes no sense. We follow all the rules and the outcomes are illogical and inhumane. So I am trying something else, and you, you listener, you are my something. Our something, I am not alone on this transcendent telephone, you can find us in the heart of the gentrified new old town, the corner of Cass and Seldon, between one gate and another. We show up at Honest John's every day between light and dark, so come and check us out, join the freak show, do the funky chicken as you go! Right now I have got to blow this psycho ward and get on down the road towards the afterglow. This is Dawud B and that's my show!"

Dawud pressed a red button on the recorder in his palm and slipped the headphones off of his head. He smiled at Dune, deeply at ease.

"How's that?"

Dune nibbled her lip. "You drove me nuts talking about a circus that had no location, no address, and no way for me to get to you. You're lucky I'm persistent."

"Persistent? You were just lonely and desperately horny."

Dune sucked her teeth. "And why are you broadcasting?"

"Because 'there's a limit to your love,'" he sang at her. "No, for real, it's because I watched *The Secret of Nimh* at a formative age and think there is some secret radical sect of survivors in a magical underground cave nearby."

Dune was quiet. Sometimes Dawud's humor was sharp enough to get close to her heart.

"I'm sorry lover ..." Dawud was watching her face closely now, aware he'd pushed a bit too far. "Dune, I'm sorry. I love that movie. I laugh at all the wrong things. I just ... We don't know if anyone's out there, and probably, they aren't. If they are, they probably aren't listening to the radio. And if we find them, it's probably going to be some crazy militia or some violent fuckers, it isn't generally the Mother Theresas roaming the streets at this point in an apocalypse."

Dune nodded, not interested in arguing. "You've watched a lot of movies. Read a lot of books. But you've never actually lived through this moment. I haven't. In every apocalypse I have ever seen, people go completely crazy and it's chaos and war. That didn't happen here. People slipped away, people disappeared, people went quiet, they went underground. No looting, no real resistance even. We had a city of hundreds of thousands and now, as far as we know, there's just us, less than a handful."

Dawud leaned towards her, eyebrows gathering, "If there is even one more person out there surviving alone, shouldn't we know that?"

Dune nodded, her face betraying the way her mind had already jumped ahead to her next thought. "I hear that, I hear all of that. But beside all of that I am sitting with, what then?"

Dawud shrugged, smiling. "I really wish I understood you more, babe. What do you think is going to happen here?"

Dune turned and looked at Dawud's sweet face. She smiled a little, letting a ghost use her mouth, "We must live and not die."

Dawud looked mock disgusted. "Well then maybe it's time to move to Key West?"

Dune opened her mouth to respond as Marta and Florida flitted across the back of her mind, and Dawud suddenly moved himself over and sat his full weight on her small lap. She had to laugh, crushed. "Hush now. Don't explain." He kissed her quickly and then stood up, pulling her to her feet.

"I'm sore as fuck. Surviving catastrophe is hard work. Let's go sit in Farmer Thorn's hot tub," Dawud smiled, setting up the recording to broadcast on loop until they came back to reclaim it.

. . . .

"No one expected it," Dawud threw back his beer, sinking deeper into the hot tub. They were playing another of his games, covering their lives like announcers at the Olympics. "These two breathless warriors might just survive!"

"His lack of athletic prowess is balanced by his gloomy wit," Dune countered.

"She's expected to slouch across the finish line," he continued.

"If he doesn't win by a belly!" She finished.

"Hey!" He growled at her.

She reached over and patted his belly, firm and round. "Yours is harder than mine!"

He grabbed her hand and pulled it lower, kissing her. She kissed back for a moment with his dick in her palm, then pulled away. She always tried to stay alert when they were outside. And once Dawud got going, he had a hard time ... pausing.

He leaned out of the tub and pulled out a toothpick, chewing it to move the energy of frustration.

She leaned over and kissed him on the nose. "Don't sulk."

He was still, a rare thing in his body.

"The survivors could have experienced many intrepid sexual adventures, left alone in a city full of cameras." He had something like a British accent now; Dawud Attenborough. "However, the female specimen was uncharacteristically prudish."

"The horny male was unconcerned with their pending doom." Dune watched the sky, then turned to him, in her own voice, "You think the cameras are still recording?"

Dawud laughed. "What, you worried about endoftimes porn.com getting a hold of some footage of my dick in your mouth?"

"The male specimen is notably crass when blue-balled. But the female keeps her grace, her beauty. Watch as she—"

There was a boom, followed by another sound.

They slipped down in the water as one, hiding, waiting for more noise. When none came, they slowly climbed out of the tub. Dune toweled off, scanning the sky, unable to see anything from the valley between buildings.

"What is it?" Dune knew they'd need to go look, but didn't want to say it.

"Not what. Who. Shit doesn't blow itself up, Dune." She wanted to challenge this—it could be a gas explosion—but Dawud wasn't arguing.

Dune pulled her clothes onto her damp body and grabbed her shoes, not looking back to see if Dawud was behind her. In front of the house, she looked up and down the street.

Dawud stepped up behind her just as she caught it. There, due southwest, was some kind of smoke blocking the stars. Dawud took her hand.

"Could be anything," she said.

"Could be nothing," he answered, scared. "I'll check the radio."

They watched the smoke rise for a while before Dune pulled Dawud into the house, feeling protective.

....

She woke up feeling feverish, exhausted. It was the darkest hour of the night and she couldn't remember her dream, but the echoes of it were in her body. Dawud was a furnace next to her. She crawled out of bed as quietly as she could and pulled her favorite of Kama's house muumuus over her nakedness.

She went down to the kitchen, tea on her mind. But when she got there, the basement door was slightly open. She went to it and looked down. The light was off downstairs. She closed the door and turned away, but then turned back, opened the door, and stepped into the darkness.

When Dune touched the top stair, a smell came drifting up to her—fragrant, wild. She moved down the stairs, spooked a bit. At the base she took a deep breath before she turned on the light. She just needed to check. She flicked the switch.

There were vines growing up the walls, and green covered every surface. Dune stepped onto the soft floor both verdant and concrete, crossing the short distance to the model. It was wild.

It was beautiful.

Dune touched the edge of the table. It seemed to vibrate against her fingers, to have its own life force. She checked on her own home on the model. The little monopoly house had windows now, with lights on inside. Leaning in, Dune saw there was a sprinkling of snow on the yard, on all the yards, over the whole city.

She stepped back and then dropped down to squat, balancing on her hands. Under the table the vines had reached down and into the ashes of Kama.

Dune laughed, disbelieving. She reached forward and touched the vines that connected her parents' detritus, so thick and sturdy.

As she looked closer, she noticed that one of the vases was cracked all the way down the side, but the vines were wrapped around it, holding it together.

"Moms?"

The basement was just quiet. Quiet and growing. She stood up and scanned the room. The vines grew up the wall, but didn't cover the faces, growing around them in curving lines. She turned to the computer, the files. The vines grew around them.

This should all be frightening, but it wasn't. Dune's back was to the model as she looked at the data, so she heard the sound before she saw the source—a scraping ch-ch-ch. She whipped around—the People Mover began inching forward on its track.

Dune's jaw dropped and she slowly walked closer to the model.

The little train moved faster and the vines that had grown around the track receded, moved, adjusted in front of her eyes. Soon the train had looped the downtown area completely and it kept going.

"Nice touch, Dad."

She sat for a while, enjoying things that could not be spoken. She looked at her own house in its small wilderness. Without much thought, her eyes moved up to Captain and Jizo's house. Wishful, she picked up the house and moved it to the empty lot across from her home, berating herself in Brendon's voice, bending the material world.

She would move it back, maybe tomorrow.

She left the basement to its magic.

....

Dune spotted the person.

She had a bag of the ganja seeds she'd saved and was planning to walk around the neighborhood until she found a good place to cast them, let them grow. Instead, a few steps from her porch, she saw that someone was standing in front of Honest John's, facing the building.

Dune doubled back and ran to the house, calling in to Dawud, "There's someone! Someone came!"

Dawud's breath caught, "No shit!" and then he was out the back door, moving down the alley with Dune in his wake.

"Slow down!" she gasped, wanting to make a plan.

"Keep up," he shot back, ducking low.

The person was facing away from them, but Dune still didn't want to move. Dawud dragged her forward out of the alley; Dune resolved to fight with him about this later. They stood quietly, Dune trying to catch the reflection in the bar's windows, taking in the short fade of hair, brown skin that had gold in it, a mid-size frame in a gray t-shirt tucked into camo pants, tucked into boots. They seemed to have a mask on.

"I heard the broadcast and came to see." The voice was neutral, androgynous and soft.

"Do you live here?" Dawud responded, standing still.

The person's body visibly changed hearing Dawud's voice, straightening, almost turning.

"Yes! We live here, downtown. We've been here. Um ... are you ... are you actually Dawud B? We don't want to fight."

Dune looked at Dawud. We?

"We don't want to fight either," Dune said, feeling protective. "What do you know about Dawud B? Why don't you turn around?"

The person stood still for a moment before responding. "Some people seem to think H-8 is transmitted through the eyes. We don't think this, but we try to respect people's fears." The person still didn't turn around. "We all listen to the Everything Awesome Circus! Together."

"That's amazing. I love that the show has been reaching you." Dawud looked at Dune and spread his hands blamelessly, smiling a bit. "We don't believe that thing about transmitting through the eyes. But hey, what do we know? I never even considered it."

Dune cut a sharp glance at Dawud's charm, slicing her neck with her hand, which he ignored. She was scanning around them, looking for others. It didn't seem smart to walk into a "we" situation.

The person pulled a walkie talkie out of their right pocket and lifted it to their mouth. "Rio, Rio calling in. Dawud B is here!"

A voice crackled back, "Please clarify. Dawud B of the Everything Awesome Circus?"

Dawud looked over at Dune with a wicked smile on his face. She tried not to roll her eyes.

Would he endanger their lives, out of ego?

"That is correct. I have Dawud B and an unknown here. Should I bring them in? Over."

"Bring us where?" Dawud asked, his hand drifting back towards his gun. The person held up a finger, listening intently to the walkie talkie.

Unknown. Dune remembered how she had felt when she first heard Dawud's voice on the radio. It had been the most wonderful, magical, and comforting thing that she had heard in forever, a ripe grapevine in a graveyard. She had walked out of her aloneness into a life with him and never really looked back.

She wouldn't question their devotion to him or dismissal of her. She knew that gratitude.

Communication came back through, staticky and abrupt. "Granted. Over and out."

Rio pocketed the walkie talkie. "I'd like to turn around now. Do I have your permission?"

Dune and Dawud looked at each other. Dune felt her curiosity cut through her, almost painful. Dawud smiled mischievously.

She knew what he felt—the moment when the adventure trumps the fear. They nodded at each other, then answered simultaneously, "Yes/sure."

Rio turned around, pulling the gray cloth mask down to show the bottom half of their face.

They were striking—Black with a freshly shaven head, full mouth, dark inquisitive eyes, wide tipped-up nose, long neck. Each feature seemed a shade larger than the space provided, but it fit together. Their cheekbones were pronounced without being effeminate. When she clocked the small rise of breasts under the gray t-shirt, Dune felt a welcome confusion; she didn't experience the person in front of her as a woman.

"OK." Dawud spoke as if breaking an awkward silence, and Dune realized he was watching her take in this stranger. She caught the smallest shiver of resignation at the edges of his mouth; she wanted to erase it. He turned to Rio, who was gazing at him in open awe. "I'm Dawud B, radio host, best living poet in Detroit, apocalypse survivor—so far. Nice to meet you."

He offered no hand and Rio extended nothing in return except a full, toothy smile. Then they said, "No wisdom, no learning, no mind, no mind at all, I am the empty minded, the clear headed, the vessel awaiting wine, and perhaps the divine."

Dune recognized the words from one of Dawud's best shows. Rio's eyes shifted from Dawud to her, still beaming. "He's been really important to us. It's strange to meet him."

Dune nodded, thinking that this would be a brilliant trap. The familiarity ... "I was the same way. I'm Dune."

"I'm Rio, of Murmur City." They didn't sound competitive. Rio looked from Dune to Dawud and back. "How y'all get around town?"

"We mostly bike," Dune answered. "Did you—did you blow something up a few nights ago?"

"No. But we know who did. We can show you."

"Ok."

Rio nodded, pulling their face mask back up. They held their hands up and stepped carefully around the corner of the bar and came back in view with their bike.

"Follow me?"

Now Dawud held up his hands. "Give us a minute?"

"Of course!" Rio propped their bike against the wall and then propped themselves against it, looking away.

Dune and Dawud crossed the street to the empty lot.

"Most likely they're gonna eat us, right?" Dawud started, pulling his smokes from his back pocket and flicking one to life.

"My spidey senses are unclear." Dune gave a small smile, balancing her curiosity against her fear. "What do we do? There's a 'we'? A whole city?"

"She came alone though. That's a good sign," Dawud looked back at Rio, who was leaning against the corner of the bar. "And she knows about the boom. You knifed up?"

"Always." Dune felt pretty sure that Rio would balk at being called "she." And she couldn't really imagine stabbing anyone or Dawud shooting anyone, for that matter, but it seemed smart to be armed.

"Mask?"

Dune patted her back pocket for the square of handkerchief she tied around her face. Dawud had a military-grade N95 mask in his bag and they both got their masks on and left them around their necks.

After a moment, Dune reached over and took Dawud's

half-smoked cigarette, bringing it to her lips. She coughed immediately; the additives intense compared to her usual handrolls. She
handed it back and, needing to redeem her cool, said, "Fuck it.
Let's go see what's up."

Dawud turned to walk back to Rio, and then stopped. "Should
we go tell Captain and the kid?"

Dune shook her head, "No. We shouldn't reveal their location,
just in case. And there's nothing they can do if we don't come
back, it will just worry them."

Dawud nodded, holding Dune's gaze for a moment. Everything was changing, right now, and she felt him grounding his
nerves on her calm exterior. She reached forward and touched his
shoulder. "Come on Dawud B, greatest living poet in Michigan.
Time to meet your fans."

....

The bike ride was quiet, moving through the streets towards the
river. Near the YMCA, Rio pulled over and put their bike in a
rack in front of the gym. Dune wondered if Murmur City was
occupying the YMCA and, if so, if she could come use the pool.
Rio turned from the bike rack and said, "Park here."

Above them, the People Mover, Detroit's strangest form of
transportation, had just rattled away. Since the 80s, the elevated
train had run a circle between the Renaissance Center, the Greektown Casino, and the stadiums. It served a purely tourist function
as far as most Detroiters went—neither Dune nor Dawud had
ever been on it. Rio waited for them in the entryway, patient.

"The People Mover shouldn't be running," Dawud whispered
to Dune. His brown eyes, bright with sun, were suspicious.

Rio heard him. "I know. It started up the other day, just

continuous loops. We aren't sure why. But we tested it and no one came, no one seems to be running it. So we're using it as a more secure entrance."

Dune swallowed awe. She remembered the train starting days ago on Brendon's model and whispered thank you to her father, for whatever magic this was.

"I seriously thought it was manually operated." Dawud shrugged, unnerved. "Maybe we could just walk?"

"They're expecting us by train."

"Train it is," Dune kept her voice light, wanting Dawud to know she thought it was safe, even though she couldn't imagine explaining why she thought that. Each day brought more opportunities to tell Dawud the specific way she'd lost her mind, and each day she delayed.

Dawud stood up and looked both ways, then darted behind Rio.

Dune had a hard time not laughing when he went into National Guard warrior mode. His tummy was soft, his shirt was torn, and he was mostly her teddy bear at this point. He had some training that made him very capable in these scenarios, but when he was doing all the official right moves for reconnaissance, it still looked like he was playacting.

Then again, it felt like they were playing Post-Apocalyptic Survivor every day, the city as their stage.

She checked both ways and followed them into the open air staircase with the small turnstile at the bottom. Rio and Dawud jumped the turnstile and Dune swung under it. The three ran up the stairs, pausing for breath at various points.

The train pulled in, all hollow and clack, stopping quickly with a jolt. The doors opened and they stepped into the last car. Rio stood holding a grab bar, Dune and Dawud both instinctively sat down.

"Are you a soldier?" Rio asked Dawud.

"Guard," Dawud responded. Rio looked confused and Dune understood it. How could someone so distinct and liberated be part of an entity that followed orders?

As the People Mover chugged out over the empty downtown blocks, they could see rolled up yoga mats stacked next to kettle bells through the big windows of the YMCA, beyond which was the tilted indoor track that had always made Dune's calves feel off balance. They crossed over the lot that once held the twenty-nine stories of JL Hudson's department store, over the tattered green awning of an Irish pub, and into the spooky casino ground of Greektown, where random fluorescent and neon lights were still on flashing.

Dune had grown up inside Kama's critique about this train and how people could get a shuttle from the airport to the Marriott, and then use this People Mover to go to a game, the casino, the River Walk—visiting the city without ever touching Detroit in any real way. This thought grazed the tender wound of Kama's loss and Dune was grateful for the mask as the small and familiar wave of grief crashed through her.

Dawud pointed as they approached the Ren Cen—there was someone on the platform.

Dune froze a bit, thinking of how the Ren Cen had been covered in green mold for months in her basement. The seven towers of the General Motors Renaissance Center were all connected into one big super structure, full of shops, restaurants, a hotel, a movie theater, banks, and businesses. The central tower, occupied by the Marriott hotel, rose seventy-three stories above Detroit, the tallest building in the state. If there was ever to be a city within the city, this was the place.

The man waiting on the platform was short and seemed older, with a thick beard growing out under his mask, his brown head nearly bald. He struck Dune as a warrior, incredibly rigid. He was turned slightly away from them, not looking at Dune or Dawud as Rio stepped off the train first and greeted him with a fist bump. They conferred quietly.

Then Rio turned back and gestured between them all. "Dawud B, Dune, this is Mohamed."

Mohamed looked at them now, nodding at both of them and pulling his mask down long enough for them to see his face, both tense and smiling.

"We welcome y'all to Murmur City. Where y'all been?" Mohamed's voice was a high pitched, gentle drawl, catching Dune off-guard.

"John R., then Second." Dawud answered easily. Dune stayed quiet.

Dune had a million questions, but knew that questions exposed as much as answers. She didn't want to give away too much right now. Dawud, feeling her quiet, swallowed his next words and Rio nodded to Dune, respectful.

"Follow me." Rio turned and walked briskly inside, Mohamed at their side. They asked no more questions, not looking behind them to where Dune and Dawud worked to keep up.

Inside the Ren Cen towers the world was deeply gray. There were places where the halls seemed to close in all around them and others where the towers opened up to stretch into a dark ether above them. The walls and staircases were thick concrete, the architecture screaming of the 1970s with girthy columns and prints on every textile. The carpets underfoot were red and thread-bare. They didn't see anyone else on their walk.

Dune had only ever been to the movie theater and the Mar-riott, and reaching both places she'd always needed a GPS. The deeper they went into the maze of bridges and hallways, the more clear she was that she wouldn't be able to find her way out without guidance. She felt nervous, an edible creature circling the sticky edges of a Venus flytrap, tantalized by the promise of sweetness.

Rio walked them up a stalled escalator and into a round of ele-vators. Mohamed pulled a card from his back pocket and waved it in front of one of the elevators. A buzzing sound kicked in, the elevator was coming to them from somewhere.

The four of them stood awkwardly for a moment. Rio broke the silence, their eyes seeming to smile. "We haven't had newcom-ers in months. Or ... visitors." They fiddled with the belt that held up their utilitarian pants.

"It hasn't been a winning social season," Dawud said very seri-ously. Then he chuckled. "So ... how big is the 'we'?"

Rio searched Dawud's eyes for a moment, hesitant, as if trying to verify whether he could be trusted.

"Seven hundred thirteen. So far."

Dawud clapped his hands together in open surprise and then took Dune's hand in his and squeezed. Dune tried to keep a poker face, but couldn't breathe—so many people! How had they found each other?

And how had they survived?

Rio looked alarmed by their reaction. "How big is your group?"

Again, a shared glance. Dune answered, "Four. We doubled recently. And Dog."

Rio's brows lifted, but Dune couldn't discern whether they were impressed or underwhelmed.

The elevator arrived. Rio's eyes darted up and Dune's followed. A camera adjusted slightly as they got on the elevator.

"You'll have to tell us how you've survived," Rio continued.

Dawud nodded eagerly. "For sure. And we would love to hear about you, too." He was looking out the elevator's windowed side, which faced the city and river to the south and west.

Dune didn't speak. She looked at Mohamed, who was contained and quiet. Then she glanced at Rio, directly in the eyes, as the elevator started to climb. Rio looked back, just as direct. For a moment it felt as if they were alone. Rio's gaze was open, their eyes massive and brown, dark freckles occasional on their cheeks. Eventually something softened in their look and Dune guessed there was a half-smile under the gray.

Dune dropped her eyes. She felt heat in her chest and jaw. When she looked up, Rio's eyes were on her body. Dune had never been so openly perused by a stranger, especially not at this thickness. Dawud had hidden his desire until they were already lovers. Dune turned to catch the view, shy. They had just cleared the city and were high enough to see the Ambassador Bridge.

"Holy fuck!" Dune stepped up to the glass.

There were visible trucks on the bridge. Below that, there was a small armada of boats floating under the bridge, at least thirty.

Dune and Dawud looked at Rio, the questions all over their faces.

Rio shared what they knew as they continued their slow, steady ascent. "They showed up three weeks ago, just one truck. Since we established ourselves here, we've focused our security on the tunnel, which is fully blockaded on this side. We are also generally watching the river, the bridge, and the perimeter established by the National Guard before they got shook and bounced. The first truck came over for just under two hours, then went back across the bridge. The trucks have gone no further than the southwest area as far as we have been able to tell. They came for a week, more trucks each time. After the first week, a barge showed up. Last week the demolitions started."

Dawud made a small "boom" sound. Dune was shaking her head. The elevator bell rang for the top floor.

Rio led the way out, eyes again looking up at a camera that shifted slightly with their attention. Dune caught it and wondered who was watching, and what they were looking for.

She looked at Dawud and he chucked his head, so she knew he'd seen it too. She felt gratitude for him, being in this with her.

"How did people come here?" Dune asked. Rio and Mohamed were walking ahead of them again, down a short hallway.

"The first citizens of Murmur City had a plan to gather in the abandoned theater with their survival packs when they got the alert. That was like a hundred people, calling themselves 'organizers.' The rest of us got lucky—some were invited, some just came because the Ren Cen seemed safe, some heard a rumor. Most people we invited joined us. Some of the original citizens got H-8, and we cared for them while they died. But mostly this space has been well."

They stopped and pulled the keycard chain out of their back pocket. "Pretty amazing given how many people were showing up ... but not recently, not in months. It's starting to feel like we're it." They flipped through a set of keycards and then pulled out a white one, holding it against the door. It clicked and they pushed it open. In front of them was a round room with views south to adrienne maree brown

Canada and west beyond the bridge, to the old factories. Rio and Mohamed stepped aside.

Dune stepped in first, walking ahead of Rio for the first time since they met. She walked all the way to the window and squinted, trying to see the trucks coming off the bridge. Dawud stepped up beside her, picking up a pair of binoculars from the windowsill. He scanned the horizon with them for a moment, and then handed them to her.

He rested his hand on her hip, in the easy way they had with each other. She restrained her desire to pull away. She told herself it was because it was dangerous to let these strangers see them as a couple, to show how valuable they were to each other. She refocused on what was in front of her, adjusting the binoculars. When they brought the river into sharp view, she was able to see the decks of one boat. She saw orange uniforms, some wearing hard hats. Everyone she could see seemed totally at ease. And white.

They took turns passing the binoculars back and forth, noticing to each other what they could see: trucks clustered in four different areas, all in the southwest, plumes of demolition dust pouring forth.

Rio waited quietly until they were satisfied that they had seen it all.

"A few floors down we have an observation station. Want to see it?"

Dawud looked eager again.

Dune felt nervous, "No eye contact?"

"I mean, most of us know it doesn't work like that," Rio said. "I looked in the eyes of every single person in my family, watching them die. I bet you did too. Masks didn't do shit either, we don't wear them in here. We just trying to respect the folks who get really

178

scared of that, we want them to feel welcome here, on their own terms. The true believers live and work further in the structure."

Dune nodded and, with little fanfare, they all tucked their masks away in pockets.

"Let's go then."

Mohamed took his leave with a friendly "nice to meet y'all" as Rio walked them down to the observation station. They entered a room with floor-to-ceiling windows that overlooked the same perspective they'd just seen. There were four people in the room. Two with sonic scanners—big satellites—facing the bridge and connected to headsets.

All four looked up when Rio entered and offered up smiles as Dune and Dawud walked in. There were all ages, from a Black girl who looked about fourteen, to the eldest, a Black man with dreadlocks that started halfway back on his head.

Rio didn't introduce the four by name, just said, "Dawud and Dune are our visitors. I thought we could show them some of our observations of the bridge activity?"

A tall, handsome Latina who offered her name as Lowra started reciting what they knew, pulling up video on her monitor. She was the first person Dune had seen here who wasn't Black or brown-skinned.

"The trucks seem to be working off of a grid system, demolishing buildings in an outward square spiral. So far nothing is being built, but materials are being developed from the wreckage of the demolished buildings which, by the way, seem to be in fine shape for the most part. The demolitions don't seem necessary, but we are still analyzing. It's hard to make distinctions, given the uniforms, but it seems there are about 310/320 workers now on board. We got some recon footage."

She flicked on a projector cube. The recording started off shaky, held by someone jogging in the direction of smoke. There were three loud bangs and, each time, the person holding the camera dropped, paused, and waited. When the smoke seemed just a block or two away, the runner seemed to slip through an alley.

What the video showed next was unbelievable to their eyes.

The camera came out from a building down West Grand Boulevard. The end of the street, closest to the defunct bridge to Canada, was packed. There were demolition vehicles covering the street about four blocks to the left and it looked like they were tearing things up all the way down to 75, the highway at the end of the road.

The workers wore orange jumpsuits with no writing on them, no less than fifty people along the wide street. As far as Dune could see, the people were white men and women, looking equal parts strong and dirty. And carefree.

"No masks. No gloves." Lowra pointed with her fingers at their bare hands.

As they watched, the video jerked closer and closer, refocusing. A wrecking ball swung across the pavement, up over the once curated trees that split the boulevard, and then back down, nearly grazing the pavement before hitting a house that looked like a pale blue fortress.

Dune had always noticed that strange little house when Brendon had driven her down Grand to the riverfront to fish. She'd loved it as a Detroit oddity. She felt the impact as the front face of the home buckled under the pressure, the wall caving inward, weakened. The ball swung out again and then back, hitting nearly the same place and crashing through this time, as if there was nothing solid in the way.

Each time the ball hit the home, Dune gasped. Even through the footage and computer speakers, the collisions were impossibly loud.

After watching the house smashed open and down, Dune was fleshing out the map of this street in her head, trying to get a whole picture. This was the fifth building from the Canada end of the street and the previous four were already in various states of deconstruction.

The camera zoomed in on a few different places. The first house on the block had a strange vehicle in front of it, something she'd never seen. It looked like a trash pickup truck had mated with a concrete pouring truck. The crushed building materials were being scooped up in a long reaching metal jaw and dropped into the open back of the mechanical creature.

And then, below, it shat out long flat boards.

Dune grabbed Dawud's wrist, needing someone near her to take in this bizarre new reality.

Another home had workers all over it, picking through the rubble for something. It was hard to tell what they were pulling out. Dune pointed them out to Dawud, who looked shell shocked.

"It's gotta be metal, piping," he whispered. "Otherwise they could have gotten it without knocking shit down."

And then, "Dune. Fuck ... "

Dawud and Dune looked at each other and around the room at these strangers. Dawud rocked back and wrapped his arms around himself.

"Whatever H-8 was ... someone thinks it's over." His voice was low. Dune nodded—no one would be in the city limits if they thought H-8 was still a threat to their lives.

Lowra bowed slightly. "Exactly. Or it was never a threat to *them* in the first place. I've never been a conspiracy theory type, but ... this shit don't add up. They're staying at a camp near what appears to be a small castle in central Windsor. We were planning to run a night recon to see if we could embed someone in the teams, but then the boats appeared and have not left. We aren't sure we can cross undetected, even east of Belle Isle. The Anishinaabeg are assessing this week and will let us know."

When the woman stopped talking, she glanced at Rio, who gave her a curt, pleased nod. Lowra sat back down at her station.

"How do you know we aren't with them?" Dune caught herself off guard with her question.

"We have a database of who's still here, identified visually at minimum. We've seen you before," Rio answered. "Honestly ... we have a lot of questions for you."

Rio gave a guarded look at the rest of the room, and then turned to a man sitting beyond Lowra. "Pull up the aerial."

In another minute, an aerial shot of Detroit was up on the screen. Dune focused on keeping her face neutral as she realized what the view showed. The city looked familiar, it's major streets like spokes spreading out from the river in a half-wheel. And there was a wild green perimeter, clearly visible from this height. There were veins of green crawling through the city and they all seem to originate from the Cass Corridor. From Dune's house.

"So. We have been tracking this growth. And ... we know it's you. But we don't know how."

Dawud chuckled a bit and Dune realized he was nervous.

She looked down, unready to put words on the work she'd been doing these months, intentionally and accidentally.

"It's cool, you don't have to explain it yet. But whatever it is, it's a security blessing on the border. One we'd never have thought of. So ... thank you."

Dune nodded awkwardly, feeling everyone's eyes on her, some suspicion, perhaps some respect.

Dawud spoke up, "Thank you for sharing this with us. Question for y'all: are your white people dying?"

The Murmur City crew exchanged worried glances. "No."

"We have a report that white people who evacuated Detroit are committing suicide in high and sudden numbers out there."

"A report?" Lowra asked.

"Yeah—I was National Guard, still am I guess. They send me data and alerts sometimes."

"You're a soldier?" asked the Black man beyond Lowra.

"I prefer poet-on-call, but yes." Dawud smiled and Dune was able to notice through her own discomfort that he was a bit on guard. She thought he was smart to show they had valuable information, too.

"I guess Dawud B couldn't be perfect," the man shot back, eyebrow raised as he smiled at the screen in front of him. Everyone in the room looked a little shy. Rio cleared their throat and some of the energy before asking, "Would you be interested in seeing more of our home?"

Dune felt ripe with questions: Would they accept her and Dawud? How much information would they have to divulge to be valuable here? How had they known to come here? What had it been like to watch the city change from these towers? How did they get enough food for this many people?

She wanted to know everything about Murmur City and how they had all survived here.

chapter seventeen

Generations

Rio walked them back into the heart of the buildings, to another set of elevators. No path was direct and soon Dune was lost again.

As they walked, Dune asked about the name "Murmur City."

"Is it because the grievers murmur when they get sick?"

Rio looked perplexed and shook their head no. They said it had something to do with one founder's love of Maya Angelou, and starlings in flight, and living quietly. "You know about murmurations? The birds, those big patterns? I can show you videos." Dune remembered the starlings on the edge of town. Rio continued, "We're trying to be like them—small moves, maximum collective safety."

The tour began in a massive room that faced the river, on a lower floor. It was a greenhouse flooded with sun, raised beds full of green growing things that Dune now recognized—kale, lettuce, broccoli—and many she didn't, even after her own gardening experiences. There were Black men gardening, harvesting, processing food in the room. They talked to each other, laughing.

Most of them didn't pause what they were doing to look up, but Dune noticed the curiosity, sideways glances. The discipline of attention stoked her curiosity.

Across from the humid heat of the greenhouse was a room that Dune could hardly see the end of. This room had no windows, but rows and rows of troughs with water in some, soil in others. Food grew up trellises from these troughs in abundance. Rio pointed out tomatoes, green beans, grapes, cucumbers, squash and what they said would become watermelons. Lights suspended over these troughs, moving slowly in a back and forth motion over the green in micro-orbits. Everything looked repurposed, used, and creatively pieced into systems, and again a handful of Black people moved confidently through the space, caring for it all.

Rio didn't respond visibly to the excitement Dune and Dawud showed around the food, but as they answered every question thoroughly it became plain how proud they were of this self-sufficiency. When not answering them, Rio mostly stayed quiet, letting them take this in.

Through a set of double metal doors were huge vats full of fish, filling a showroom that was two stories high, its temporary walls retracted into pleated vertical piles. "There's trout here, catfish there, tilapia there," Rio pointed out, letting them peek down into the water to see the masses of fish in motion. "We repurposed part of the TCF basement level to grow chickens and goats. There's not a lot yet, but it's just a matter of time."

"TCF?" Dawud looked confused.

"Cobo Hall? They renamed it after a bank from Minnesota." Rio shared this with annoyance, which Dune felt too—the constant renaming of things was one of the patterns of gentrification in the city. Although, in this instance, she was glad that the monstrous building of cold, endless hallways no longer uplifted a long-dead racist's name.

She felt Brendon and Kama on her shoulders, watching, listening. This was what they had talked about, what Wes and Mama Vivian had talked about. This was self-sufficiency.

She had been scrounging in grocery stores and strangers' houses for nonperishables, trying to figure out how to manage all of the gardens in her neighborhood to yield more food for them come spring. Jizo had been stealing canned food from pantries. But here in Murmur City, they were off the grid and not even reliant on the weather for their fresh produce.

Dune filled with a hunger much larger than her belly.

....

Before they left, Rio let them know they were welcome to return any time and ask any questions. Dune hardly slept that night. She wanted to know if this place could be safe for Captain and Jizo, safe to visit, maybe even safe to join one day. She wondered if they could be part of it, but still live in their own home. She wasn't in a rush, but also couldn't imagine staying away.

Luckily, Dawud was waiting with coffee when she woke up, ready to return to Murmur City. They boarded the train around noon and Rio met them at the People Mover entrance of the Ren Cen, which Dune found somewhat mysterious.

They were learning the extent of Murmur City's surveillance. So far it seemed like they knew every time someone boarded the train. Dune wondered if they knew every time she and Dawud left home, or if anyone moved in the city.

Rio took them into a public space in Murmur City. They followed a different path through the shadowy center of the towers and then walked into an open atrium where there was sunlight, and people sitting, reading, writing.

Two Black kids, maybe four-years-old, came running up and wrapped themselves around Rio's legs. Rio's face lit up as they squatted to talk with the kids, a different self coming to the surface for them.

"Tato Rio, did you know that caterpillars aren't scared of heights because they never even *think* about flying because they don't even *know* they are butterflies?" The first one spoke, a girl, eyes round with wonder, voice sure of its rightness.

"They are 'maginal.' Just like us!" The second one fumbled the big word, but got it out. He smiled and it lit up his small face.

Rio smiled back at the two. "Well, where is our cocoon then?"

"Here!!!" The kids yelled, arms thrown wide. Rio laughed.

"I like that. Who told you all of this?"

"Mama Lacie! She said we need to have some butterflies in the garden." The little girl again. Rio adapted a face as serious as that of the children.

"I agree completely. Maybe my new friends have some butterflies where they live?" Rio looked up at them and Dune couldn't help but smile as the kids got excited.

"Hmm, did you say butterflies?" Placing her hand at her chin dramatically, Dune thought for a second. "Oh yeah! When it's warm outside, there's definitely some butterflies in my backyard."

She smiled, covering a flicker of fear. Kids had been evacuated early in the sickness. How were these babies here? And how were they safe? Were they all special, angel babies like Jizo?

Rio stood up and the kids swirled about them as they stepped further into the atrium. There were a lot of people in the room now, mostly Black people. This was the most people Dune had been around since before evacuation. With tender surprise, she realized she recognized a few of them. They were her parents' people.

She felt embarrassed, she felt late.

The room's interest in them was palpable, but Dune experienced no trepidation. Whatever test had been required to enter this place with more people in it, she and Dawud seemed to have passed.

Rio softly gathered peoples' attention with a double clap. "Murmurs, I'd like to introduce our visitors, Dune and Dawud B. They'll be around sometimes, please help them feel welcome."

The room was quiet just a half-second before shouts of welcome and some waving of hands. Dune noticed that several people lit up upon hearing Dawud's name. A few people looked at her in new ways too, perhaps recognizing her as Kama's daughter—thicker, changed surely by grief. She smiled through her nerves around how she was being perceived. Rio led them to a table off to the side, clear that they were not to be bombarded.

In the center of the space was a round wooden table covered in food—sliced bread still warm. Small bowls of butter, vats of steaming soup. There were jugs of water on each table in the room, too. Dune started formulating a question.

"We filter it three times. So far, it seems to be working." Rio answered before Dune could ask. "Just in case, we purify it."

Rio walked them through getting a bowl, some of the spicy pureed butternut squash soup labeled Orange Porridge, a big slice of seed-filled bread labeled Motown Multigrain, smeared in butter. At the table they each got a glass of water. More people were pouring into the atrium and Dune felt a lot of eyes on their table, but no one joined them. Only kids ran around them, multiplying until there were twelve, fifteen kids in the room.

Dune wanted to see Jizo play here one day. It felt so unexpectedly safe, this deep in the coils of a building that had always been a no man's land to her.

....

"It was Kama."

Dune was back for the third day in a row and she and Dawud had shamelessly aimed for the midday meal time again. This time they had plates piled with fresh greens, so crisp and bright that Dune, after her winter of frozen foods and soups, felt emotional. And there was a curried fish salad to scoop onto the plate. She was sitting between Dawud and Rio, her eyes trying to document every detail of the room in front of her while also listening to Rio talk with an Anishinaabeg elder named Bineshii who had joined them, the first adult to do so. Hearing her mother's name snatched her attention to the elder, who looked impish and ready to talk story.

"Kama insisted we have this plan, just in case. She held the session where we all packed our go bags. We joined the Alliance for Justice because of her, you know. I wasn't on the Survival Committee with her, but I know she drafted and presented the proposal they made, which led to the Alliance ordering a lot of the materials and supplies, especially the seeds."

This was news to Dune. She knew her mother had been in meetings with various community projects all the time. When Brendon was alive, the dinner table had often included a review of various organizations and meetings, as well as some vibrant debate about the direction things were going, especially when Mama Vivian had been over for dinner. But after her father died, Dune couldn't remember much of the content or organizing permeating the field of grief in the home. There was silence, there was scarcity, there was sadness.

"She stole the key—well not stole because fuck ownership! She kept the keys to Cobo and the Ren Cen loading docks, back then, after the social forum." Dune had been a kid when Kama worked as an organizer for the US Social Forum, when thousands of people had gathered for conversations and panels on the topic *Another World Is Possible*. Kama had handled local logistics. "She said racists don't check on people they perceive as janitorial," Bineshii laughed, a sound like a flock of birds moving together up and out of her body.

"Kama had equipment delivered here, stored in a room the building considered obsolete, there's still all this printed shit from the forum stacked down there. You know how she was with information," Bineshii danced her fingers around her crown of wrapped braids, "Everything was in her head. She said 'the probability of an extinction event was getting too high not to have a plan.' So we had a plan. When we get a text or phone call that says 'Maroon time,' we meet at the old theater here in the Ren Cen with our go bags."

The elder's voice and eyes softened. "We didn't expect Kama to go first."

Dune bit hard, tightening her jaw to the point of pain under the pressure of emotions that she wasn't ready to show. She wanted to know all of this. She needed to know it all. But she didn't know what to do with it. She didn't know how to sync up this Kama from Bineshii's story to the depressed and dysfunctional woman that Dune had fed and cared for, tolerated and loved, lost and burned.

Bineshii gave Dune a sad smile, and Dune felt her unspoken boundary touched, honored.

"Listen," Bineshii leaned across Rio to grab Dune's hand. The elder's hand was strong and bony, her eyes quick as embers. "Whenever you are ready, you come out to Belle Isle. We are reclaiming all of Detroit as a sacred space, taking all our land back into our stewardship. But we are thinking about how you all can be here in a good way. I come here as a liaison. Your mother is a person we honor greatly. Her spirit embodied the Teachings of the Seven Grandfathers. We will sit in ceremony for her, with you, when you're ready."

chapter eighteen

Home Conversations

Jizo's face was moon bright. He bounced through the precarious door of his and Captain's home and hugged Dune, then Dawud. He grabbed both of their hands and dragged them through the kitchen, the sink full of dishes.

He pulled them both into the living room.

"Y'all two had us awful worried, huh Jizo!" Captain patted Jizo's head as the boy sat on an ottoman next to Captain's comfortable seat. "I hope you were up to no good!"

Captain was giving them an easy time of it, but Dune could see the relief in his system. Dune felt ashamed. She had been wrong not to tell them before going to see Murmur City and then they'd just gotten immersed in exploring the world of people and experimentation occupying the Ren Cen. Captain and Jizo'd had no way of knowing what had happened to Dawud and Dune when they hadn't biked over the past few days.

"I'm sorry, Captain," Dune said. "We're going to leave you a walkie talkie today and show you how to use it to reach us. But we have some pretty big news. There's a community of people living in the Ren Cen! They made contact and we went to check them out."

Captain's eyebrows raised. He didn't seem pleased.

"People in the Ren Cen? Hmph. What kind of people are they, young lady?"

Dune swallowed her desire to speak to the absence of ladies here. So far it didn't seem to land on Captain when she lightly suggested his behavior was regressive. She would need a more pointed and private talk soon. For now, she focused.

"I think it started with some people living downtown and some activists who'd been planning for a while. Mostly Black people, but they all seem immune to H-8. When they realized they couldn't stop the virus, they moved into the Ren Cen to avoid getting evacuated. Other people heard about it and followed suit."

Dawud added, "Before we even got here they had secured a year's worth of food and they're growing stuff right there on site. They have medical supplies—they feel confident that they can sustain up to a thousand people. They showed us their, what was it, Forage Board. Got stuff from all over the city."

"Well now. Living there?" Captain clacked his teeth in and out of socket as he pondered this. Dune and Dawud nodded, both trying not to be overly enthusiastic. "A bunch of people just up in the Ren Cen, huh. Black people?"

Captain had specific ideas about what Black people would and wouldn't do. His lens was a particular Blackness that had limitations from trauma, and royalty as the only lineage, and liberation as a future state.

"Well, mostly Black people," Dune said. "I did see some others."

"I have been very curious about, you know, who stayed and who left. It seemed all the white people left, but that's not necessarily the case, it's just about who we got to see, when the news was still coming locally. They wasn't in the street, I'll tell you that."

Captain leaned back, contemplative around his own words.

Dune shared more. "Captain, they have been surviving there. Over seven hundred people. They're growing food, they have a whole way of operating. They're keeping track of the borders— there are people doing some kind of construction by the bridge, that's the explosions we heard."

Jizo nodded while Captain's eyebrows popped up. "What explosions? What they find?"

"We saw them. It's a bunch of people in uniforms knocking over houses in Southwest and flipping them into replicators." Everyone looked at Dawud, confused. "Sorry, blerd joke. Stargate? Anyone? Replicators are this alien species that eats everything and copies itself until there's nothing left in the universe. Eh. Like, it looks like a massive 3D printer on a truck?"

This didn't clarify anyone's confusion and Dune couldn't clarify without laughing, which she suspected would just make it all worse.

"They haven't figured out anything yet, not really," Dawud continued, emptying his pockets onto the kitchen table in a nervous tic. A pocket knife, folded pieces of paper, smokes, a ball of cash. "They know a little more than we do. We can't tell who the trucks belong to; friend, foe, neutral. It's not looking good though. Like, why are they processing the raw material of these buildings into some other substance to build with? What is that stuff? Murmur City don't know. And in terms of H-8 ... they have theories, I would say about an equal number as us."

"There were also," Dune cut in, "children and I think some kind of schooling system. Children Jizo's age."

Captain laughed. "Shit, Jizo ain't Jizo's age."

Dune nodded her agreement, but added, "There are kids to play with. There is a lot of room. There is water and food. And there is safety, more than here anyway, especially if there's folks coming over the bridge. They have a watch that takes turns keeping the place safe."

Captain had a smile on his face as he listened. "Mind if I ask why you sound like you have a used car behind door three my dear Dune?"

Dawud laughed really loud at that. "Captain, we think we should consider joining them. Dune especially thinks that it would be amazing to go and be in their enclave, which is a young, strong, capable enclave."

"There are 713 people there. They are making a new world." Dune tried to sound neutral, but she wondered if Dawud sensed that within the excitement she was repressing was a growing interest in Rio. "No more scrounging and sneaking around town. If those trucks come down Mack, we're fucked. Sorry ... screwed."

She tried not to use language around the kid, even though she wasn't worried about him ever repeating it.

"Ok I hear that, safety in numbers. How'd they all end up there though? Don't no seven hundred people just accidentally have food stored up. Some cult shit? If it's too good to be true, they probably tryin' to kill you. And why would they let *us* in? What's the trade off?"

Dawud was smiling again. "It's my brute strength, Captain. They need strapping men up in there. And actually, everyone just thought Dune was the sweetest person they'd ever met."

Now Dune blushed hard. "They are all fans of Dawud B's podcast."

"His what?"

"My radio show."

"OK now. Must be good."

"It's incredible," Dune affirmed. "And ... we are survivors, Captain. I think that's the most interesting thing to them. Surviving means we have some combination of luck and skill. It's totally reasonable that they would want to pull in as many capable people as possible, no matter how old. Or how young."

"They need every possible hand, every possible finger, at work," Dawud kept his face so serious, Dune couldn't tell if he was teasing her or her own mind was finding subtextual content to feed her guilt. "We are going to visit again, probably tomorrow. Depending on how things go—we want you and Jizo to check it out eventually."

Dune knew this wasn't about Rio for her, this was about the possibility of being around people, being part of a community. She'd tried so hard to make it alone. Dawud, Dog, Jizo, and Captain—they'd all shown her that she missed contact. Love, care, friendship, sex, parenting ... It didn't much matter to her right now what happened in between takeoff and landing, the content was almost irrelevant. Being around other human beings was the intoxicating and necessary part.

"Jizo." The boy looked up at Captain, eyes wide and expectant. Dune found him a joy and a discomfort to be around. "You heard that? We could go live downtown with some of the other people still making a life in Detroit."

Jizo was noncommittal. He looked back and forth amongst the adults and around the house at large.

"I am not saying let's move in there," Dune kept her voice light, low. "I'm just saying that there are other kids there, people all of our ages. You could learn with other kids."

"Riverfront property!" Captain held up his fist.

Jizo smiled at her, looking both older and younger than she'd ever seen him. He looked up at Captain and leaned closer to him, looking sleepy. Dawud spoke next.

"Man, we can literally do anything we damn well please. Jizo, you can go to school. Or not, whatever. The point is that we have been alone here, and then we found each other, the two of us, the four of us. That mutt. And here we have 713 other fucking humans who are not dying or scraping by."

"You sure it's seven hundred?" Captain whistled.

"That's what they said," Dune answered. "And they are surviving. With each other."

Dune knew the people they had met were important, but she didn't know if it was her body or her mind, her gut or her heart having that feeling. "We'll keep talking about it. This is our decision, we will make it together."

Jizo popped up and ran over to hug her. She had said what he needed to hear. This made her feel the particular tenderness of wanting a moment to last forever, him holding her, the crook of his dimpled elbow smashed against her mouth.

She was suddenly exhausted from the late night and all the excitement. She bowed out to bike home and had slept for hours before Dawud slipped in beside her, having stayed and talked to Captain until both men's eyes were crossing.

....

They were standing in a massive crowd of people, none of whom

Dune recognized, all facing Captain's house with its burn scars and picture window. Captain's face filled the window, larger than life, as if he was a giant trapped inside his home.

Everyone was chanting, spittle flying and fists in the air.

There was a shuddering of the world and a great cheer went up from the crowd. Then Captain's house lifted up, seeking balance on unfolding legs, moving randomly, like a fawn. When the house was upright on four long trembling legs, people in the crowd started dancing and someone kissed Dune on the cheek.

She turned to see who it was, but the house began walking.

Everyone looked at her expectantly. The house itself paused and Captain was watching her. She began the awkward journey of guiding the house around the corners, under the trees, down the wide streets designed for a booming car industry. All the way to the lot across from her home.

The house walked onto the lot and lowered itself slowly down onto the overgrown grass. It looked like it had always been here.

....

The next visit to Murmur City spooked Dune.

A woman approached her, Dawud, and Rio near the elevator bank, coming too close. Dune recognized the old activist as someone Kama had always been wary of, a troublemaker, truth-teller, trickster; Kama had hated tricks. The woman went by Mama Rue and she drew near, presenting a sweet Black face with a million folds along the surface.

Mama Rue pointed at Dune, poking the air between them as it were an invisible force field. Dune wished it was, especially when Mama Rue started speaking:

"What chu see, girl? How they speak to you? I know you see

'em. I know you gather 'em into you. I know you know what I'm saying to you, girl. OK maybe not *girl*, even I can see that." The old woman smiled and her teeth seemed longer than expected, and still her gums were showing—a truly massive mouth. As Dune studied the woman's face, she suddenly felt a deeply rooted fire ignite, a strange arousal. Mama Rue was not beautiful, but she was fine—fine in the crook of her smile, fine in the ease of her brow, fine in the confidence of what she shared. Now, looking in her eyes, Dune saw she was timeless, strong, vibrant.

"You not special here, you know. Least not by way of magic, we all magic here." Mama Rue gathered her eyebrows as if in consternation, but she was smiling. Without seeming to move, she tapped Dune's temple and Dune tensed up, felt Dawud coil next to her. Rio made a calming gesture, gently pushing Mama Rue's wrist down and away from Dune. "Ain't you figured that out yet? The dirty trick of all of this? You die or you get a gift, some obtuse enhancement, to survive. You ain't gotta hide that. Magic don't even seem to last much once you find your tribe. You only special cause you Kama's baby! No one else here has that distinction, she in you."

Mama Rue searched Dune's face for traces of Kama. Dune knew, from her own explorations of that path, exactly where her mother marked her face. She had Kama's deep, dark eyes, wide tall forehead, a mid-cheek dimple which showed up for skepticism more than laughter. Where Kama's face had been bold, Dune's was delicate, but Kama was there. With their eyes locked, Dune felt that Mama Rue desired her, body and spirit. And desired her mother within her, and every mother before that—and Dune couldn't deny the overpowering feeling that she wanted to lay down and time travel with this stranger, who felt more like a deity.

"We thought you died. We thought you must've got it from Kama, thought you was gone. But then, folks start sighting you around and we confirmed your survival at the rescue center at Wayne State. 'Looking for eggs,' that's the sign of someone who's alive and making plans. Once we knew you was alive, was just a matter of time 'fore you'd need people. So we kept an eye on you."

Rio guided Mama Rue away and as soon as the elder was facing a different direction, Dune saw a small old woman where the ancient sensual god had been and Dawud wrapped an arm around Dune's shoulders. He spoke into her ear, "You can explain later. About the magic."

She tried to move out of his arms, but he held her steady. She stopped resisting his offer and let him hold her.

chapter nineteen

Homing

In a rare moment of stillness, Dune sat at home, alone. Today felt different, she felt different. After months of quiet toil as a caregiver and then months of silent unwinding in solitude, Dune could not now put her finger on the desire to be alone. She had always reveled in seclusion, in looking ahead at a day with no plans, or an evening with no expectations. But this virus had pushed her beyond her capacity for loneliness. Now she felt at odds, to not be with Dawud, or Captain and Jizo, or meeting people at Murmur City.

It was her birthday. March 25. She'd been due April 2, but came early and, according to her parents, easily.

It was her birthday, but everyone who knew that was dead or gone.

Dune opened the cabinets and then the freezer, to see if she had anything that could pinch hit for a cake. There was a box of Magnum Ice Cream bars, chocolate ice cream dipped in a chocolate-almond frosting that hardened on the outside. Dune ate the ice cream bar while watching herself in the front hallway mirror.

Her hair was wild and frizzing around her face, it had been a week since her most recent braids, which Dawud had done under duress. The edges of her face were soft, blending with her neck with no indication of territory. She wore a red dashiki and some sweatpants. She still felt the shape of masculinity in her bones and jaw. Being masculine wasn't something she ever had to perform or project, it's just who she was. But that undercurrent was perhaps the only aspect of herself she recognized under the shape-shifting influence of her quarantine life.

Without fanfare, Dune walked into the kitchen and grabbed a pair of scissors. In the hall mirror, she cut off her braids, leaving a hacked halo that she expected would curl when she next showered. If not, she'd shave it off. Her mother had believed hair held energy. Dune was slowly learning that everything had energy and that some of the energy responded to her intentions. She carried the braids down the basement stairs and laid them between the vases of Kama, an offering to the people who created her.

Dune finished her birthday ritual and flicked on the radio in the kitchen.

"Join us after these messages for an interview with Dr. Natasha Rogers from Detroit, and hear her allegations of serious misconduct around H-8."

Dune turned the volume up, doing dishes as she waited impatiently through a round of commercials. Who cared about hair products? Who cared about floss sticks?

Finally the show returned, the host a slow speaker, enunciating as a form of torture.

"Now, Dr. Rogers, please tell us a bit about who you are."

"Well, my name is Dr. Natasha Rogers." Dune recognized that Black competence. "I was in Detroit at the beginning of H-8. I actually witnessed patient zero come into my emergency room and I didn't know what to do. I'd never seen anything like this virus. So I've been researching and researching for months. And I can now confirm with no hesitation that H-8 was a man-made virus that was released in Detroit as an act of biological warfare."

The host gasped and there was some mumbling. "Are you saying that an act of terrorism decimated one of our greatest American cities?"

"Yes, Sam. Domestic terrorism, most likely, white nationalist terrorism. While it's unclear if the intention was to kill all of these Black and Brown citizens of our city, it is absolutely clear that this virus did not occur in nature. What I have discovered is that the virus suppresses serotonin—almost into non-existence. I suspect, best case scenario, that the virus was meant to just be a simple serotonin depressor. But in people already depressed ... it overwhelmed the system."

Dune was gripping the sink's edge with soaped up hands, shaking with rage.

She dried her hands and turned off the radio after the interview ended. Stepping into the center of the kitchen, she covered her mouth, thinking of her mother, her depressed mother who was trying so hard to get a routine, to be upbeat, to fake it til she made it. Up against a man-made virus that stole her chemical joy?

Kama hadn't stood a chance.

. . . .

"Dune!" Dawud was shaking her awake in the morning half-light. She felt bleary, sore, bewildered.

"What, Dawud, what is it?"

"Uhhh. I ... uhhh ... come here," he pulled her up from the bed, over to the window. Across the street, in the heretofore empty lot next to the Thorn's place, was ... Captain's house. Which, for the previous forty years of its existence, had lived 1.75 miles northwest of the parking lot. It was only part of Captain's house. The top floor of Captain's burnt-out house was sitting amongst the grass and weeds on the empty lot.

Dune was wide awake in an instant. "It worked!?"

Dawud's eyes were on the house, stunned. It took him a moment to hear her. When he did, he turned to her, frowning, "*What* worked?"

Dune grimaced, almost comically, caught but too shocked for defense. Then she yelled, "Are they *in* there?"

"Shit!" Dawud responded, moving towards the door in a panic. He nearly fell down the stairs and then ran, barefoot, into the cold street, Dune right behind him.

In the window of the house, Jizo stood, his hands against the glass, smiling.

"That fucking crazy kid!" Dawud exclaimed, circling around to where the back stair had been. He touched the knob to open the door and then stopped and knocked. The door opened a minute later and Jizo stood there, giddy.

They followed him through the house to where Captain was standing in the kitchen. For a minute, there were only shouts of surprise and disbelief. Dune had never played so dumb in her life. She felt speechless, but also like, if she spoke, she couldn't help claiming this miracle as her work.

"I mean ain't this something? Ain't this *something*?" Captain rubbed his hands together.

"Did you feel it?" Dawud asked.

"Didn't feel nary a thing!" Captain said, looking at Jizo, who tilted his head to one side as if falling asleep in that instant. "Went to sleep in the North End, woke up in the Corridor, now this is a miracle. A true miracle!"

Dawud looked at Dune suspiciously and then walked around, placing his hands on the walls, the cabinets. He wanted to assert some control, or at least reality. "We don't know if it's structurally sound. We are going to need to thoroughly check it out before y'all stay here."

Captain and Jizo agreed, and let themselves be led out of the house, over to sit on a very muted Dune's porch. Dawud pushed at the house, checked the foundation, went inside and jumped up and down. He found nothing tremulous. After every test he could think of, he came to sit with them and look at the half-house. "Wow. This is some shit."

Jizo was unfazed, climbing on the railings of Dune's porch. Captain couldn't take his eyes off of his transported home. Dune felt a shiver up her spine, hearing his in-breath, like time had just slowed for a moment.

Captain said, "The house looks like it's always been there! Happy birthday to you, Dune!"

Dawud cut his eyes at Dune, "Birthday?"

"It was yesterday," she told Dawud. Then turned back to Captain, "But how'd you know?"

Captain shrugged and pointed to Jizo, who just smiled and curtsied.

"That why you cut your hair off?" Dawud asked.

Dune nodded, "I guess, yeah."

"Well I think it's quite becoming, young lady," Captain began.

Dune cut him off. "I don't feel like a lady, Captain. Or a girl, a

207

miss. You can use other terms of endearment, but please don't use ones like that."

The old man looked offended, pained. "Oh, I … I didn't mean any harm, I—"

"I believe that. Deeply. That's why I am telling you. We neighbors now. We are in this together. So I just wanted you to know when you say that, it throws me off, doesn't feel like me."

"Ok. Ok I can try that on." Captain still looked contrite, but at that moment Jizo did a full back flip off the porch railing, sticking the landing. Satisfied when they all gasped and warned him to be safe and praised his bravery, he ran back up and did it again, until the tender moment had passed.

....

Dune woke up early and listened to the house. Total quiet except for the soft snoring of Dawud next to her.

The day before, as the impossible had slowly become undeniable and, thus normal, Dune had avoided questions by convincing Dawud and Jizo to forage an apartment over on Lafayette, the home of a rich friend of Dawud's. He'd been musing over the ethics of raiding the home of someone he knew. Dune said she thought a true friend wouldn't mind, if they ever returned.

She had found really good high thread count Egyptian cotton sheets, unopened in a linen closet. Rich people. Dawud hit the jackpot, a freezer with lots of frozen meat, including eight rashers of bacon. It didn't look like there'd been any interruption in the power source, everything in the freezer was in good shape. The meat was wrapped in white paper and written on.

When Dune saw that, she was excited—it was likely from the Cass Corridor Sausage Company. The good stuff.

Dawud was just happy to have meat, since neither of them had been ready yet to cross the line into hunting and skinning things. When they'd discussed it, it had turned their stomachs, the idea of roasting squirrels over a pit. Pheasants? No. Dogs? Absolutely not, although Dawud had a whole theory about small yapping dogs being closer to rodents than mammals. For Dune, that made them less appealing, for Dawud, that meant the guilt might be lessened in the meal.

"But I'll let you know when I get that apocalyptic," Dawud said, as he often did when she brought up various survival activities they should learn. Hunting, recycling water, even helping her make jams and soups for the winter. "I'll focus on keeping us safe. You feed us. Tarzan Jane shit."

He kept them laughing like this. She didn't mind his commitment to food being a magical unseen process, because he was always down to go into dark flooded basements, shadowy spider-crept attics, kitchens with people decomposing at the table. The places that still shook her a bit, he barreled into, fearless.

On a bacon day, it all seemed very fair.

Now, she went downstairs and entered the kitchen, her eyes carefully avoiding the basement door.

She moved around the wide space, cooking, feeling the sunlight pressing through the blinds. There was a child in the house and an elder, a lover and a dog. She felt at that moment that even if they hadn't found any one else left in the city, if it was just these three humans, this dog, and her, she would be ok. It was a family. With magic.

Dune started boiling water for polenta. She was grateful for the frozen butter they'd found, but missed Gruyere cheese. There was no other way to get quite that flavor.

She pulled out the bacon and decided to cook a whole rasher for the four of them.

As she cooked, she made a case for herself for why she didn't need to return to the basement. She would probably never find another person. There wasn't really more to do with the data she'd gathered. She'd been planning to scope out the wild places gone fertile on the model, to see if there were other people still alive out there, or other places growing wild along the edge of the city. But all along the Ren Cen had been green for a reason. Couldn't that be enough?

She caught herself, feeling dishonest. What she was really planning was how to hide the magic from the boys.

She stood over the popping bacon, feeling like she'd been cheating and was going to have to confess.

She didn't know how to tell Dawud about moving the house, the border of bones, the tenacious green in her basement that indicated life in the city. Or the near patterns she had heard in the words, the number of people whose last words were names that she could only assume were loved ones, or activities she associated with joy.

It was like trying to speak the beauty of the natural world—it was too mysterious to tell it.

The smell of the bacon filled up the house, waking her boys.

She'd put Captain and Jizo in the office for the night. Dawud wanted to be absolutely sure Captain's house was solid before they slept there again. As Dune put sheets on the pull-out futon, she'd wondered briefly if they needed separate rooms, if they would tell her of their needs. She felt no red flags about Captain and Jizo, even if their story was an odd one. So far, her gut had been the most trustworthy guide in this game of survival. She'd felt affirmed late last night, passing by the office where the door was open and the two were sleeping deeply, back-to-back.

Now they emerged from the room, Jizo leading Captain with gentle eagerness. Once Captain sat down, Jizo started poking around, drifting near the basement door. Dune put him to work setting the table.

Dawud came down the stairs, shirtless, shorts belted under his tummy, durag still tied tightly around his head, white athletic socks pulled up his legs, flip flops. He said he was born in Detroit, but sometimes she saw other places in him, L.A., Oakland, El Paso.

They sat around the table, quiet at first.

"Listen, I know that y'all might be feeling very focused right now on the how of all this," Captain waved his hands to generally indicate his house moving through time and space. "And I get it. And there is a how, we not all hallucinatin', something peculiar and miraculous has happened and we the only four might ever know about it."

They all looked at each other around the table, Dawud's eyes lingering on Dune's face as her eyes avoided him.

"But I remember when I was born." This brought everyone's attention sharply back to Captain. He had a slightly glazed look on his face. "I remember the darkness and then suddenly the light, so much light I couldn't open my eyes for days. So much sound and some of it coming from me and my own lungs! To my mind, it was a miracle.

"And I remember being five, six, seven years old. I remember jumping into the back of a truck with my brothers, waving at my momma, then going to pick cotton in a field all day long. At the end of the day I got less than a dollar. Then one day the man who owned that land? Up and died. And his daughter decided the land should belong to us who worked it. My family had a plot of land and we pulled everything out that dirt. For us, it was a miracle.

"I remember coming home one day from work and Delilah looking in my face and understanding without my saying a word that I had been broken that day. The way she scooped me up onto her breast like to carry me to justice? There was a certain kind of light, the sun itself had to shift when Delilah touched my heart, the warmth poured back into me, even though nothin' had changed about them people disrespecting me.

"Black people know how to get out the way of misery. When we want to. I can't speak to it scientifically, that's not my ministry. But the spirit of Black people? The way we persist as a joyful noise? The creative process of survivin' America? There's always been a virus after us here. Different forms, sho, but it's always after us. But. You can hate us, make H-5011 and we still gonna be in the sun."

They all sat quietly, filled by his words.

"Ok well, don't just sit there now. Let's eat!"

Captain reached to make his plate, and Dune laughed, then Dawud, and Jizo was smiling.

This felt good. They needed exactly this.

. . . .

That night, before she slept, Dune found the key to the basement door in Kama's desk. She locked it.

She didn't want to go down there and was scared to touch the model again. The power to rearrange the world was too tempting. And she sensed that Jizo was drawn to ... the work. And whatever he was, boy, angel, ghost, gift, he had plenty of magic in him.

She wasn't ready for him to slip into the basement and find the mystery there. He would disrupt all that was real in the name of playing.

There was too much she didn't understand. Even if he could help, she wasn't ready for him. It was her inner place, her little sanctuary, her mother-father place in a dead world.

She didn't know how to hear what the green was saying, but she was sure that for now the message was just for her. She put the key on a string, diving her head through it to create a long necklace. The weight just under her breasts was comforting, like she carried the city in the safest place she knew.

"So we gonna talk about that, or nah?" Dawud was waiting up in bed for her.

Dune looked at him without answering and then pulled her shirt off in an overt move to distract him.

"Nice. But nope. Did you make that house move?" Dawud sat very still. Dune looked at him, belly suddenly trembling. If he didn't believe her, it would break everything. She mostly didn't believe it herself, but she couldn't hold his doubt on top of hers.

But ... it was true.

Dune crawled onto the bed and faced him. "I think so."

Dawud was so still that Dune almost spoke again. But he finally said, "And the overgrowth. On 8 mile, around the city. That you, too?"

She was surprised. "Yes. I mean, not me, the model. Down in the basement. It keeps growing and growing. Every time I move something down there, or change it, well ..."

"So you thought it was OK to just move their house with them in it?" Dawud looked stormy.

"I didn't know, I didn't know that it was actually working.

I didn't know that I—" Dune stopped. Some part of her had known it was possible. She had just gone with her gut, she hadn't thought about all the details, about all the dangers. "I didn't think it through. I just, I just did what I wanted."

"Well. Be more careful." Dawud held for another moment. Then he reached over and pulled her in for a hug. "Baby, that's your magic!"

She let him hold her. Muffled into his shoulder she said, "My magic?"

"Yeah, like you know how something comes over me when I'm doing the *Everything Awesome Circus*? That didn't happen before. I don't know where that stuff comes from, it's just in me. It's my magic. It's how I met you and now it's led us to Murmur City. So you, you got the basement."

It was easy, how he said it. She had the basement. No big deal. He pulled her down with him and was snoring before she could expound on how insane it was, she was. His acceptance, the fact that he could sleep next to her, made her feel a bit less ashamed, a bit more ... witchy. She had the basement.

The next morning he woke her up saying something about Rio.

"What?" Dune's eyes were bleary. She felt defensive.

Dawud was propped up on one elbow in the bed, hands rubbing his belly.

"Sorry." He wouldn't look her in the eye, even though his voice sounded light. "I just want you to be true to yourself."

"I appreciate that." Dune rubbed her face. She couldn't get used to how Dawud just brought everything up. "And that includes you."

"But I'm not attracted to Rio!" Dawud said quickly and then smiled a little, willfully misunderstanding. Dune felt her defenses collapse in her, faced with his insecurity. She scooted closer and leaned against his shoulder, joining him to rub his belly.

"If you met an interesting guy right now, what would you do?"

Dawud turned his head and kissed her crown. "Negotiate."

Dune slid her hand down his belly and under the sheet, taking hold of his morning erection. "Hey," he pulled her head back by the hair. His voice got soft, pivoting into a 1930s radio accent. "Women will drive you mad. Better to get a safe little choir boy."

"Greedy, raging woman of the night. She even smokes grass!" She pulled at him faster, pressing her breasts against his side.

"She is a black hole men enter and never escape!" He pulled her thigh onto his lap and walked his fingers up her softness and into her.

"Fuck you, baby." She said, laying back.

. . . .

Dog was sitting in the living room when Dune came down, well worked and relaxed. Dawud was even more enthusiastic a lover since she'd cut her hair off. Dog's tail started thumping the ground as she came closer and he stood up for a head rub.

"Don't you look so happy, sweet sweet Dog."

Dog spun around in a circle, seeming like a much younger and wilder creature. His dignified face was playful, grinning.

Dune crouched down in her scratching and at some point, the petting became a hug. She was hugging Dog, and she could feel that Dog was with her, in the hug and also in the joy of having formed a little family out of his strays. The completion was the five of them. Wherever they went from here, they would be going together.

chapter twenty

Murmur City

Dune was in Murmur City. It was dark, but there were lights shining up from the floor. Big ferns hung down from above, so she had to part them in places to move through.

She moved through a thick curtain of ferns and Rio stepped in front of her. Dune felt an immediate tension in her thighs.

There was nothing to explain. Rio brushed their cheek against hers, so soft. When their mouth was closest to her ear, they whispered, "I just need to feel it."

Rio started kissing the small spot at the base of Dune's left ear, just under the lobe. Everything lit up. Dune was trying to breathe, to swallow. They grazed their palms up her arms, holding her neck briefly, turning her head further away so they could kiss more of her neck.

Dune felt all of her attention in the points of contact, a spinning up through her scalp and alarm signals exploding down her belly. She stood very still for a moment, as if she could possibly be innocent. Then she reached up and touched Rio's chest, pulling the soft heft towards her until only the nipples were between her thumbs and middle fingers. In this way, she pulled Rio in and they collapsed easily together against the wall.

Rio was fast, but gentle, slipping their right fingers along the band of Dune's jeans until they found the button, inched down the zipper. Their hand turned, palm against Dune's belly, fingertips inside her boxer briefs. Dune stepped her legs apart, fingers still pulling and twisting gently at Rio's breasts through the soft cloth of their t-shirt, taut desire obvious.

When Rio's fingers reached Dune, they slowed down, or time did. Rio spread their pointer and ring fingers with a little pressure, opening Dune up. Rio's middle finger slid in, rubbing back and forth along the messy slit where Dune's entire life was happening. Up over the clit, down, circling the tight place where Dune could be entered, but not entering, coming back up to the growing bundle of pleasure sensors that unmapped her body.

"Please," Dune's voice echoed through the jungle.

Rio smiled at her and kissed her on the mouth, deeply, for the first time, at the same time she slid one, twelve, a hundred fingers into Dune. Her moan filled Rio's mouth as Rio moved their hand to touch every place where Dune could feel. Then Rio stopped kissing her and put their left hand over her mouth. They leaned close and looked in her eyes, and then started pounding their fingers into her, building up a feeling so good it brought tears to Dune's eyes.

Dune woke up to find she was slippery wet between the thighs, breathing hard. She knew that she'd been dreaming of Rio. As Dawud snored, she brought herself to a quick orgasm, fantasizing about kissing Rio's soft mouth for the first time, over and over.

....

Dune and Dawud returned to Murmur City for another visit, following the now familiar process of biking to the People Mover and stepping out onto the Ren Cen platform. This time there was a blond woman on guard, who turned away when she saw them.

Dune didn't think they'd seen her, or any other white people, on their previous visits. She said, "Hi, I'm Dune and this is Dawud B."

"Permission to face you?" she asked. When they said yes, she turned around. "I'm Gloria. Just a minute."

Gloria announced the arrival of VIPs 1 and 2 through her walkie talkie, and then led them inside. She leaned forward as she spoke, sloping her neck and shoulders. Dune wanted to tell her to stand up straight.

"Y'all not worried about those people seeing you?" Dawud asked as they followed Gloria into the labyrinth of the Ren Cen.

"We don't make it easy. No lights in the outer rim at night. No daytime patrols since we saw them." Gloria paused for a minute. "By the way, I'm a huge fan."

The subsequent gush, telling Dawud in detail about his impact, lasted the rest of the walk as Gloria took them up a few escalators until they reached a different, smaller atrium. Rio, Lowra, and a few other familiar faces were working quietly around a table with strangers. They all looked up, welcoming.

After some small talk, Rio turned to Dune, "You mentioned having a kid in your number. Could I give you a tour of the school while Dawud gets a security debrief?"

Dune didn't know if they should split up. She looked at Dawud, who inclined his head to her, a teasing smile at his lips. He turned away and asked Gloria a question about the debrief.

Dune interrupted briefly to kiss Dawud on his cheek and then let Rio lead her off to the school.

First, Rio escorted Dune to an office that had windows looking over the sun-dappled atrium and a section of standstill escalators. Rio stopped in the middle of the small room and turned to Dune, whose mouth went dry as she looked at them.

When Dune liked women, it wasn't usually androgynous women. She was drawn to soft femmes, round bodies, swinging breasts, soft bellies, dimpled thighs—bodies that moved in a lot of directions when they walked.

She couldn't tell yet how Rio identified, but intuited femme was no part of it. They were straight, long, a mirror of Dune's former body.

"Who did you lose?" Rio asked, making direct eye contact.

Dune held up one hand, fingers spread wide. As she spoke she folded her fingers down. "My mother, H-8. My grandmother, natural causes. Elouise and Lou, H-8. My ex, Marta, abandoned the city. A sick person I played hospice for. Everything. Everyone else left."

Rio nodded, working their lips.

"And my fear of dead bodies." Dune held their gaze. "You?"

"My partner of three years. My partner's child, he was seven." They paused, holding eye contact while grief came and left their face. "My aunt, who raised me. Everything."

The silence filled up with their ghosts.

"Why are you still here?" Dune's voice was softer.

"Still breathing? I don't know. But I can't believe it's random."

Dune nodded. She felt similarly compelled by the massive scale of the loss. It couldn't be random, who'd survived.

"You?" Rio leaned forward a bit, searching Dune's face.

"They're all still here. Everyone I love is here." Her hands lifted up, presenting the ghosts that always haloed her memories these days.

Rio smiled a bit at that, eyes going soft.

"And Dawud?"

"He came later. I love him." Dune felt shy and happy saying it.

"Is it exclusive?" Rio kept a very neutral face.

"Oh—no." Dune closed her eyes a bit, gathering clarity. "It's been unexpected and wonderful. And we are both gay as fuck. So—we are learning. Learning as we go."

Rio was nodding, hands behind their back.

"Good. That's good to hear."

"And ..." Dune held the note, unable to maintain neutrality.

"Me?" Rio tipped their head back, cheek softening faintly towards a smile.

"Mmhmm."

"There are people I love here. I share space with someone, my apocalypse partner. I belong to no one and don't plan to." Rio looked down for a moment and then back up, bewitching eyes in full effect. "I'm good at love."

Dune's eyebrow lifted. "Good." Now they held her gaze, and she did not waver. "Are you ... what ... how do you ...?"

Rio laughed at Dune's stumbling. "I say gender non-conforming. I use they, them, but I don't get angry if someone says she, or he, or whatever. I'm all of the things. And I like women."

Rio stepped close to Dune at that and stood there still, letting the heat between them flare up. Dune felt déjà vu; she had been close to Rio before somehow. Then they walked past her to the door. She waited a step and then moved behind them, feeling a sweet tingle in her jaw.

Seeing the classrooms, Dune felt overwhelmed. The rooms

were deep inside the towers, with windows onto the open atriums where daylight spilled down, but no way to look outside or be seen.

Each room had books, art supplies, toys, chalkboards, and students. There were no teachers, just chaperones who made sure the children were kind to each other, encouraging curiosity. The kids could basically do whatever they were interested in.

These people were so friendly, open. Dune was struck by the overwhelming Blackness and also by the feeling that those who weren't Black walked easy. No one seemed to be in charge, but they were all getting a lot done.

The kids asked Rio to read them a book in the youngest classroom. Dune wondered if Jizo would find this interesting, if this room could compare to the freedom and responsibility he'd been carrying. Perhaps getting to play would be a relief.

They stepped into a classroom with students who looked to be middle school age. A brown boy had instructed everyone to sit on their left hand. Eventually there were groans of discomfort and laughter as people's hands fell asleep. Rio checked to make sure Dune was paying attention.

The kid said, "Ok, so you see how your hand can fall asleep so fast? Or your legs if you sit a certain way too long, like when we meditate?" The kid shook his own hand. "And now you can't feel what it's doing? And it feels so weird and uncomfortable as it wakes up that you wonder if you can even take it?"

The kids laughed and screamed affirmations.

"Well that can happen to people's morals and values too. For white people, coming to this country made their morals fall asleep. And they did a bunch of things—like imagine if your hand was asleep, but stealing everything in sight and hitting everyone around you! And now they are waking up to what they did. And it's *very* uncomfortable."

Dune was impressed, wishing her parents and Mama Vivian could witness this moment, this kid and the classroom in his capable hands.

After the tour, Dune and Rio came back to what Dune now recognized as the eating room, or one of them anyway. She hugged Dawud easily when they reconnected and whispered about the school. After a hearty lunch of dal and a chicken curry, Dune noticed that several of the adults led the children out of the room, or just drifted off themselves. Those who stayed were faces she recognized.

Her heartbeat sped up, growing alert. There were a dozen people still sitting in the room, and they slowly made their way over to the table where Dune and Dawud now sat across from Rio, joining with smiles and small waves.

"So. The Mbongi Council convenes." Rio splayed their hand out flat, palm upwards, and then curled it into a fist. The others repeated the motion. "Mama Tazina brought this idea back from her organizing work in the Congo with Black Organizing for Leadership and Dignity. Mbongi is a Kikongo word that means coming together to understand what we face, generate solutions and create strategies for collective action."

The elder that Rio nodded to was grinning with approval. She had a child's button nose and bright cheeks under a close cut fro, and when she spoke she directed her words to Dune and Dawud. "That's right. True liberation is not about slipping your sovereignty from another's grip, but taking responsibility for your own life and choices, individually and in the collective. This is not a body of power over others, but a circle to speak and reflect on the

223

values of the city. Weavers," here the elder looked around, and a few hands went up as people claimed their collective title, "bring topics to our open meetings. Anyone in the community can attend and those who vote are any who are willing to be accountable for the decision. It's good to welcome you."

Dune felt the name and face touch deep in her memory of her parents' world. This sweet-faced elder was Tazina Clark, a poet, organizer, and, as she introduced herself, the arts counselor of Murmur City. There was a mischief to her, as if she was trying not to giggle. "Y'all got questions?"

"Yeah. What the fuck *are* y'all? Is this the best cult ever?" Dawud clapped his hands together, laughing in genuine disbelief. Dune felt responsible for him; couldn't he hear how loud and jocular he sounded amongst these serious folk?

"Sister Ajana, youth council." The speaker touched her heart as she offered up her name. She was a young Black woman, slender and serious, her hair in two massive wild locs sprung from the top of her head. She spoke with precision. "We aren't a cult. We are Detroiters who had a plan."

"And what *was* the plan?" Dune asked. Was this all of it? Occupying the Ren Cen til some mysterious plague clears?

"When disaster overcomes Detroit, we stay. If possible, we find our future here." This from an Asian elder named Hoka, who Dune remembered as a respected adversary of Mama Vivian. She was an old school butch, short and sharp faced, white haired and calm in a vest that seemed made of pockets. "We have learned everything we can about staying, planning where we can live. Place. Plan. And there are other cities, but this is the heart."

Hoka nodded. "Kama said we needed to get ready, she foresaw all the small ways the city was escalating for a different level of land grab. We never thought they would take it this far. We never imagined any of us would be targeted in this way."

Dune felt slightly bruised by Bineshii's claim that Kama had been involved in this, mostly because if it was true, it meant that she had left Dune out of this, and how could her mom leave her out of survival plans?.

Mama Tazina stepped up, touched Hoka's elbow and spoke, "We have reason to believe H-8 was, is, man-made. This has recently been corroborated by a doctor who has been doing the morning shows."

"Dr. Rogers? Natasha Rogers?" Dune asked.

"Yes, that's the one."

"She was the doctor, when my mom ... she was ..."

"Ah, yes. Well—her case is compelling. It aligns with our conclusions. But it leaves us in a real predicament, because who knows what else is coming and if they could redeploy the virus. But we want to build trust with you, and share what we know."

Dune was having a hard time swallowing. Every time her mind grazed the idea that her mother's death had been crafted, forced, intentional—it felt like her brain fogged with rage and confusion. She felt Dawud lean a bit closer to her and appreciated his bulk and presence. She hoped he felt as grateful as she did at this show of trust from Murmur City. Dawud responded, "We had heard some early reports of this. We have also heard that the virus seems to have a latent impact on white people's will to live."

No one responded with surprise to this and Dune felt the channel clear between them all.

Mama Tazina walked over and sat down next to Dune, taking her hand. She spoke and it felt like no one else was there.

"Everything changes and changes again. Mama Vivian and Baba Wes were part of seeding this place. They always said to us, 'If I can't see what you are creating, I'm not interested in watching you destroy.' It was one of the only places where Vivian and Kama aligned, though they disagreed on the how. Kama thought it would take preparation and protest. Mama Vivian thought it could come through running our folks for office. Brendon was our cartographer, you know. When he died, Vivian and Kama stepped back from things. Then Elouise was going to bring you in. But ... then things just got too dangerous."

"I'll say." Dawud now. Dune was grateful that he spoke, so she didn't have to, so she could just feel the calm that was coming from Tazina's truth telling, her touch. Dawud continued, "I came home with the Guard ... Man, we had no idea y'all were over here! Didn't get the Underground Railroad bat signal at all."

The council shared looks at that one, ranging from guilt to amusement to annoyance.

Dawud continued, "What other cities have plans? Do y'all know more about these trucks?"

Another shared look. Then Hoka spoke, this time more measured. "We know more about the trucks and boats. We know more about you, we know you have connected with others. We know the *Everything Awesome Circus*. We also know we are all just beginning to know each other really, to know each other now."

Dune wanted to know everything, immediately.

Sister Ajana was soft spoken in a way that made others quiet themselves to hear her. "But we begin by listening. We will share and we will show and we will ask you questions. Our intention is to have no dangerous secrets amongst us. Let's build relationships, so we can learn if you are of us, or friends to us. Either way is ok."

. . . .

Dune asked for directions to the bathroom and was pointed to the hallway at the far end of the room. Excusing herself, she moved in a fog of processing all of the information that filled the time and space of Murmur City.

As soon as she stepped into the hallway, she felt a presence. There was a Black woman almost in the shadows, smiling at her. The woman stepped forward so that light caught her face. It was Mama Rue, looking diminutive and elder, but somehow not old. Her brown skin was dappled with freckles of light; she was small and moved easily. She stepped directly in front of Dune and slowly raised a hand and placed it on Dune's chest, directly over her heart. Dune tried to step back, but Mama Rue moved with her until her back was against the wall. Dune couldn't tell if Mama Rue was going to kiss her or speak to her, just that the elder's lips were full to the edge of ripeness.

"The lost ones are in between. They need guidance and ritual to join with nature." The woman's eyes were open and her face was that of someone speaking reasonably.

"Huh?" Dune responded, trying to bring attention away from the feeling of warmth and delight where Mama Rue's hand touched her. The old woman's eyes fluttered, closed but seeing something.

"God needs no translation, Dune. Anyone who tries to stand between you and God is perpetuating a lie. Especially if it's a man. Being a witch is being unafraid to interact with God, partner with God." Her eyes opened and looked at Dune with accusation, soft-ened by a slight smile on her pursed lips. "You've been building altars, haven't you."

Dune wanted to run away, but where the woman's hand

touched her chest it felt like they were of one flesh. She was pulsing between her thighs, she was having a hard time breathing. She shook her head, "No, my dad made the model. It's toy pieces and—"

"Child, everything is made of earth, which is made of stars. Even if we manipulate the materials into some seemingly new existence, it's just form. A stack of Barbie doll heads still has supernovas and dinosaur bones in it. And you have been working altars, manipulating earth."

Dune felt chilled and caught.

"Oh, hey Mama Rue," Rio stepped up behind Dune, gently catching the hand that Mama Rue had nearly embedded into Dune's heart. They clasped the elegant and fragile hand between theirs, giving it a charming kiss with a curtsy.

"Rio! My husband does not approve!" Mama Rue blushed and demurred. She shot Dune one more serious appraising glance and shuffled off. Dune felt as if the temperature dropped. She had to remind herself to inhale, to stay and not run after the elder.

Rio leaned in and whispered, "Her husband died a decade ago, but he is by her side at all times."

Dune smiled, still trying to reclaim her body, herself in this moment.

"You ok? Mama Rue is our Eldest and can be really intense. She means well."

Dune nodded, but she could tell she wasn't convincing Rio. She smiled awkwardly, not willing to reveal anything the elder had spoken. Rio laughed at the unspoken boundary and led them back into the atrium.

....

The next time she went to Murmur City, Dune asked Dawud to stay with Captain and she brought Jizo with her. She wanted to know how this place would feel to him. She also trusted his gut to let her know more about these people.

Walking into the schoolroom for children four to six years old, Jizo looked around, cautious. Dune squatted down to talk to him.

"You don't have to do anything here. But there's some interesting stuff if you want to check it out."

He nodded, not smiling. He looked more like a child than she'd ever seen him look. "And if you don't like it, we can go."

He held up a hand, as if he was listening for something. A child across the room laughed and Jizo looked over, face giving no sign of interest. He looked back at Dune. She shrugged. Maybe he could go laugh with them. Maybe that would be fun.

He took a few steps away from her. As he slowly approached the crew of Murmur children, Dune felt a different kind of grief—had this child never played with other children? Had Jizo's whole life been survival and care?

As he stepped up to the other kids, a Black girl with extravagant afro puffs turned around and started giving him orders without missing a beat. "Hi. You gonna be the lizard. She is the fly, so she's going to fly around the room and then you have to catch her cause you're the lizard. And then if you can catch her, then I will catch you, because I am the hawk. And then we'll see if Ron can catch me, he's the jaguar, so not technically a superior predator, but you never know. Ok?"

Jizo nodded.

"Do you talk?" the girl asked directly, eyebrows curious behind child glasses.

Jizo shook his head.

"That's ok. To be the lizard you can just hiss or make your mouth like this," And she took on a ferocious face.

Jizo looked back at Dune for a brief moment. Then the gamester yelled "Go!" and the girlfly started buzzing and squealing and ran away from Jizo. Jizo hissed and rolled his shoulders, taking on the role of lizard and chasing the girl. He was a marvel, jumping up and over obstacles on all four limbs, darting down towards his prey. He caught her quickly and then flipped around to orient as the girlhawk spread her wings and started cawing magnificently, chasing Jizo. He stayed low to the ground in his lizard role and his evasion was skillful, but just as the hawk was reaching the edge of her playfulness, Jizo let her catch him, giggling wildly in the hawk's talons. They only had a moment before the boyjaguar growled and all the kids started running.

When Dune took Jizo home, she could feel how he had adapted already to be part of the circle of children.

The next day Jizo woke up wanting to play again and Dune found him on the porch when she stepped out. She was happy he felt this way and asked Dawud to stay with Captain again. He looked a bit suspicious this time, but she shook her head.

"I'll let you know if anything happens with Rio. I won't sneak off."

For this he gave her a flurry of kisses on the forehead.

Jizo's hands on Dune's hips as they biked together through the empty streets was a distinct bliss. She was no one's mother and he was no one's child. In some way, though, they were cut from the same magic.

When Dune and Jizo's train pulled up to the platform, Rio was standing guard and openly happy for the surprise of their arrival.

They got on their knees to check in with Jizo, easily falling into conversation with his faces and sweet miming motions. Dune let them connect and watched how Rio moved, the ease and confidence in their bones.

"I was going to take him by the school for a while," she said, when she felt restless. Rio looked up, having forgotten everything but Jizo. Jizo had that effect on people.

Rio nodded. "Would you be open to talking with us, while he's in there?"

Dune felt a bit on edge at the idea of interacting with the council without Dawud. She knew she would trust him to meet with them without her. She also knew she was sitting on bigger secrets than he was and hoped they wouldn't press through her defenses. She carried her magic as an unwieldy gift.

Once Jizo was settled, Dune followed Rio to a different atrium, nearby. The walk had a quiet sparkling energy and Dune thought of several questions she wanted to ask, things she wanted to confess. None of them came out. This sort of internal fumbling under external silence was Dune's clearest flag that she had a crush on Rio, something more than a primal or pheromonal reaction.

It was distracting.

The Murmur City Mbongi Council was there waiting and convened around Dune, smaller this time. Dune was struck by how open everything was—a meeting, yes, but open to anyone walking by. Just like last time, she expected that people would pass by, pause, and listen before moving on. Council struck her as an organic process more than a role to play.

Hoka opened her hand, palm up, and then made a fist. Everyone repeated the motion.

"Any questions?" Hoka looked around, the circle was quiet.

"What is that?" Dune slipped into the silence, mimicking the fist with her hand.

"Oh!" Tazina laughed, "It's like our call to order."

"From many threads of thought and life experience," Hoka held up one hand and pointed at each finger, "one whole." She closed her fist.

"Power is in the whole," Ajana said. Dune made the fist a few times. Ajana added, "When we finish meeting, we're supposed to do this," and the girl held up her fist and opened it moving upwards, like she was tossing a dove, "but we forget."

"No one likes to give up power," Hoka spoke seriously, but others laughed and Dune caught the small, brief smile on the elder's face. "We have been talking about whether you all could become a part of this community eventually. Dawud, we had to really think about. We don't put much faith in the military minded, but we do love a good militant. He seems to be rooted in this latter category."

Dune nodded, begrudgingly. She trusted Dawud, she could vouch for him by now. She just wished he were here.

"And as for you, Dune—"

"Dune, I have a question for you." The middle aged man who spoke was slender with a bulbous tummy, meticulously styled in jeans and a blazer, with a head full of thick blond hair. Hoka gave him a poisonous look and then, with her hand, conceded the floor. "I'm Edward. You mentioned something about data when you first came?"

Dune had only mentioned that once, in the elevator, and only to Rio. She thought of the shifting cameras, of transparency of information, and what community meant here.

"Yes. My father made a model of Detroit." Dune pictured it now, fecund, overgrown. "Since the syndrome started, I have tracked each sick person I came across. Like, where they were when they got sick, what they were wearing, when. And mostly, what they were saying."

"And what *were* they saying? I couldn't pull anything from the nonsense, it's like interpreting someone's dreams or memories. We sat with each of the sick people here, hoping the words could help us flip a switch, get them back. Impossible!" Edward ran a hand through his hair, a small look of disgust over his face. "What did you figure out?"

Other council members shifted a bit when Edward spoke, asking and answering in one breath. A few of their faces reflected how Dune felt inside: he was annoying.

She wondered how to respond. Something new was coming together in her mind as she spoke. "It's memories of happy times that they've lost ... I think ... it's the memories."

The councilors looked at her expectantly. Dune shook her head, the realization simple after so much time parsing the patterns, looking for clues. She'd seen past it, missing it until this moment of accounting.

"They—everyone gets caught on something that has already happened. The words are all memories." The others looked at each other, puzzled, patient. And inside that, Dune was unraveling a knot, wanting to be careful to say what she really meant. "I have been trying to understand the pattern. This might be too simple but—I think the words might be a way of getting caught in memory, pulled from life into the realm of what has already happened. Perhaps, to live, we have to stay looking forward."

"Well, surely we have to keep a balance. History cycles back around." Hoka spoke, sure-footed. Dune could see where she and Mama Vivian had bumped heads.

"Sure, a balance," Dune acquiesced. "But things have been so hard in Detroit. Everywhere. Maybe H-8 made people think the good stuff was all behind them, behind us."

A few council members looked at Ajana then, and the girl nodded, but didn't say anything.

Instead, Rio weighed in, "I get that. We talk about that in our mediations." They looked around and others nodded. "That we cannot get caught in the past events—even the immediate past. It isn't possible to heal if we just keep processing and reprocessing, or declaring a singular history."

"Can we see this model?" Edward again, interrupting with a confused look on his face. Perhaps the memory idea *was* too simple. Dune felt embarrassed at having gotten so excited about it.

She couldn't imagine visitors to the model or how to explain what was growing in her basement.

"It doesn't travel," Dune said. "Maybe sometime I can take y'all on a field trip." She built a bridge for later crossing.

Then Mohamed spoke up, his voice high but velvety, his tone earnest. "I think it is important that we capture this wisdom that Dune is sharing with us, which is larger than the material world she has been tending. What I hear her saying, you saying, sorry," here he turned his warm brown eyes to her and she wondered how she ever thought he was a warrior, "is that time is water. If we don't let it flow, if we become a dam against it, or try to reverse its course—it breaks us."

Dune nodded, gratified to hear her ideas made poetry in his mouth. Now someone who had stopped to listen raised her hand. Dune noticed her and tensed up, in her periphery she noticed Edward and Hoka seeing the woman and getting quiet.

"Mama Rue," Ajana said, standing up to make a place for the

elder to sit. Mama Rue didn't move towards the open seat, but instead moved towards Dune, until she was close enough to touch her. The woman touched Dune's shoulders with her hands, which showed an age that hadn't reached her face.

Dune was caught in the eldest's eyes, which she'd avoided since their earlier interactions. There was a slight green in the brown pools, they seemed open just a tad too wide. Mama Rue started smiling.

"What you have shown us, shared with us—it confirms what we were feeling, intuiting, the visions that have come to us. Our beloveds, they got caught looking back. And they left us to grieve here, in the present. Time is continuous, a circle that is always equal parts behind and ahead of us. Each person is responsible for carrying some of the balance, the load—for each historian there need be a futurist. Not formally but, in terms of focus, in terms of where the life energy flows."

"Thank you, Mama Rue!" Edward tried to interrupt, but Mama Rue ignored him. Just as Dune was thinking the woman seemed more rational than before, Mama Rue's hands came up to gently cup Dune's face, then her eyes floated up above Dune's head. Mama Rue entered a trance state that made Dune think of Dawud, channeling. It occurred to Dune in that instance that what she felt around Mama Rue wasn't pure desire, but pure erotic aliveness—the woman was life itself. She was liberated life force.

"I remember during the genocide, the soldiers were children. The soldiers were children and the adults were being murdered because this tribe, that tribe, could not be tribe. Because power is the tsunami that inhales and then blows down everything. When all the village was walled by bones and there was no one older to see—when there was no getting older—they stopped moving or fighting or doing anything, and they spoke their mothers' names.

"I remember during the Holocaust, at Belzec, there was a sadist and it is a lot to say that given the work they were up to. There was a sadist and he never let us be inside, the water was thick with murk and he never let us touch each other. One day all of the children would not get out of bed, they just lay there looking at the ceiling, or the bunk above them, dumbstruck. The Nazis took all the children to the ovens that day. And the next day, everyone, no one, could get out of bed. Their bodies stopped the pretense because it wasn't living, it wasn't living!

"I remember being a slave; fifth in a line of Marys, but really seventh generation slave without a real name. And something like this happened—longing for a past that is too far to see, unable to comprehend a future. At the same moment, in the field and the kitchen and the driving wagons, everyone went away from their bodies. The whites thought it was a rebellion, they fought to bring back the workers, it was so much money just standing there staring into space, but they could not beat it away and they could not wake us up.

"I remember being on death row in Suzhou, oh. I was so guilty! I had a million excuses, but in the end it came down to fear, I did something horrible because I was tired of always being afraid and made to feel small. And they left us each alone. They kept a guard there just to keep us from speaking to each other and they gave us no books, nothing to write with, no way to apologize. Just knowing some day, like any other, we would be shot against a wall. The future disappeared from view. And one by one we left our bodies before our scheduled deaths.

"A plague doesn't happen to a person, it happens to a place, to a time, to a generation. And it's always a great depression, such a time. A black hole opens in time, a black hole is a moment where there is no future, only time pulling us back, which is in. Life is ever expanding, but with great suffering we contract, we become a vast interiority.

"History repeats itself, this is true. But it is not only history, it is also the future, all of time, all of existence, cycles and cycles in more directions than we can comprehend—like wheat, like waves, like wind. And if we lose touch with the cycle, the motion, the future, we can get caught, looking back.

"You have survived because you have every reason to look back and to surrender to history, but you have kept the flame of the future alive inside of you. You have been in the absence of fire and warmed yourself by imagining the match, the heat, the shhhh sound, and you made a pile of kindling in your belly, and you stacked wood all around your root, and you got so hot you had to step back, turn your ass to the fire, ha!

"We are no longer looking back here, we know the history, we are the history walking. We are not looking at America now. We are looking beyond it."

Mama Rue took a breath and Dune was breathing with her, tears streaming down both their faces. They were surrounded by quiet adults who, for a moment, had been one body. The eldest released her grip on Dune's face and stepped back, jaw slack, her lips rounded again into a smile. Ajana stepped forward and took Mama Rue's hand and walked with her, not leaving the room, just moving. Rio moved close to Dune, asked if she was ok.

Hoka was also watching Dune, eyes sharp, waiting.

Dune felt entranced. Transported. More than ok. She felt like she was finally in a real place, an honest place.

"I think that's enough for today," Hoka said. "From one, many."

This time they remembered. The council held up their fists and tossed their invisible doves up and up.

....

Dune waited a few days before the next visit. She wanted to integrate the experience of Mama Rue, wanted to cool off her Rio feelings, wanted to spend some time with Dawud, Captain, and Jizo.

On the fourth day, she knew she also wanted more of her questions answered.

She woke Dawud up in the pre-dawn light, shaking his shoulder as it curved away from her. He came to urgently, sitting up in alert mode and then lay back down when he saw her face. Her sleep-thick voice spoke, "I want to ask them more about H-8. I think I'm ready to know."

Dawud looked at the clock. "Roughly what time do you plan to ask them?"

Dune scowled at him. "Come on."

When they got to the People Mover platform, Mohamed was standing guard. They greeted each other and Dune asked who would have the most accurate information about H-8. He told them to wait a moment and called HQ on his walkie talkie, speaking in a code Dune couldn't follow.

Ajana showed up a short while later, alone. She shook Dawud's hand and then gave Dune a slightly awkward side hug. Dune was caught off guard, given how shy the girl seemed. Dawud looked over at Dune, some skepticism showing on his face. Ajana led them to a sitting area not too far into the building, a little circle that looked out over another empty atrium, the gray darkness heavy. She pulled out a small recorder and a projection cube, and set them down. She looked nervous.

"Before I start, there's something I should tell you. It might make you less likely to believe me." She looked from Dune to Dawud and back. "I'm nervous. We had a lot of conversation amongst the council, about how to share this with you. So I'm honored to be the person who gets to do so. You can ask me anything. We're still learning about it too."

She paused again. Dawud leaned forward with a serious look on his face, "Too much build-up."

They all laughed a bit, though Dune could see that the girl was still very nervous. "When H-8 came, it didn't affect everyone the same way. Some people got really sick and they couldn't recover. My grandmother was the one who took care of me most of the time, my parents had a hard time with all that. I was sleeping at Gram's house, on the couch. I woke up and she was just standing in the middle of the room, facing the front window."

The girl's voice shook and her eyes filled with tears that she didn't release. Dune could see Ajana in her mind's eye, waking up to that.

"We couldn't get her to come back. My uncle got scared and he packed everyone up to leave. But I didn't want to leave. So I gave my cousin a goodbye letter for the family. When it was time to go, I hid until they left me. And while I was hiding, I touched … I touched a bush? In the yard? And, boom, I could see my grandmother. She was moving into the house, real young. Like, she was my momma's age, but she just had my grandma's face. Everything was different, the clothes, the car. Even the house was a different color, it didn't have the front porch like now. And it's like, I was the bush, watching."

Neither Dune or Dawud made a move to enter the space between Ajana's words.

"It freaked me all the way out, like I almost ran back to get my uncle, to get out of here. But I wanted to see more of my grandmother." Ajana blinked, her eyes still brim full. "So I touched the bush again and just watched. Like, so much time passed. I watched her come out of the house and she was pregnant and happy. Then one time, she was on a gurney, bleeding between the legs. Then with my grandfather, he was carrying her into the house. And then she was pregnant again. And I saw my mom, as a little girl." Ajana was just barely here now, her face slack as she was transported into memory. "I started touching all the different bushes and trees around the house, they all had other angles on these stories, I just had to see more. I must have looked a fool, but who cares, everyone had left. So I just watched my family."

Dune felt familiarity with this longing and then a jolt of jealousy for Ajana's magic.

"Hoka found me. I was kinda going wild in the yard. Hoka helped me understand my mutation. Now ... I can see what Detroit has seen through any green witness."

Dawud was incredulous. "That's wild!"

Ajana nodded, half smiling. "Hoka kind of figured it out, when she tried to get me to leave the yard. I wouldn't go, I kept grabbing everything alive, asking if she could see Grams. So she said we didn't have to leave. And she came and stayed at the house with me until I told her what I was seeing. Hoka was the one who figured out that H-8 changed everyone, but in different ways."

Dune and Dawud both kept their eyes on Ajana.

"So when we came here, the question wasn't ... do you have a mutation, but more like what is it? Part of it was figuring out exactly how people had changed. Some people don't even know yet. It's not random, we think it's like something already in you got enhanced." Ajana was looking at them now, curious. Dune thought of Dawud, the poet, able to channel some kind of divine verse. But what was her something? Being a daughter? An introvert? A caretaker?

"One guy, he was really into mushrooms, something he calls journeying with mushrooms. H-8 made him able to hear the mushroom networks underground, the same way I can hear the green plants here. But he can also communicate with them. They think this might help us talk to New Orleans, Atlanta, DC. Maybe even Oakland.

"Hoka had the idea that maybe I could use this sight to figure out what had happened." Dune felt a thrill. Ah Hoka, Dune thought, not sure how long it would have taken her to get there, as even now she flailed about in her *mutation*.

"We did these missions. If there was anything alive and green in the space, I could see, I could find the memories. When I saw something that seemed relevant I would describe it to Hoka and Tamara, this amazing digital artist. So we have made this project that kind of gives you a visual of what I've found so far. Can I show you?"

Dune nodded, looking at Dawud, awestruck already. She was moved by what Ajana was capable of and by the anticipation of yet another layer of data—organic data. But she was even more impressed by how matter of fact the girl was about what she, and all of them, could do.

Ajana pressed play on the cube and a small hologram popped up, an aerial photo of Detroit. Ajana's recorded voice came on, "Six months and seven days before the H-8 Syndrome."

Ajana spoke the sound of the letter H and slid it into the 8, so it became "hate." Dawud looked at Dune, made a little mime of a bomb blowing up in his hand. Ajana's recorded voice said, "This memory is from a spider plant in an office overlooking Campus Martius." The image shifted to a sketch of three men standing in front of a window, overlooking the river.

"Soon they aren't going to want to be here at all. All they will see is their own failure." Ajana's recorded voice was flat. "It's kind of like ... depression in a bottle. They're lazy, it will just forward press that attitude. And if it works in Detroit, I've got people lined up for it." The perspective shifted and now the men stood in front of a projection screen, moving through images that flipped by too fast to fully register, leaving only an impression: Black people in factories and driving vehicles, Black people in protest.

The hologram went briefly dark, then came up with a sketch of an apartment, a kitchen, fancy, spacious.

"Two months, fourteen days after the first instance of the H-8 Syndrome." Ajana's voice returned through the projector and Dawud took Dune's hand. "Captured by a tree fern in Indian Village." The image was like a comic book picture of two men, one in a suit, the other in sweatpants and a sweatshirt. The sketch moved as the man in sweats punched the other one in the face, knocking him down on the couch. The man who'd been struck held up his hands in defense, staying down on the couch.

He yelled with Ajana's voice. "The Blacks have deformed your perfect fucking virus! They're dying out there!"

"That wasn't the plan." The man who spoke cowered down, blocking his face with his hands. "It was supposed to make them docile."

"Docile! You fucking douchebag, we've got blood on our hands here."

"There's *less* of them. Wasn't that the point?" The man on the couch sat up a bit, his tone withering in spite of the moment's brutality. "Come on. Come on—beyond optics you don't really give two fucks. They aren't here."

The man in sweats rained down another storm of punches, saying, "No one's here! You. Ignorant. Fuck. I didn't want to kill them." Panicky breath. Then, "Can this thing be contained? What can it do to us?"

The man on the couch spit blood from his mouth. "Sometimes you sound like you doubt your superiority."

"I doubt your science. This thing is mutating on you. They said some white people got it."

"Impossible. They're of African descent, even if they don't know it. That's not on me."

"You piece of shit. What if I have that same fucking strand of DNA? What if you do?"

"I don't."

"You fucking shit!" The beating continued as the sketch faded to black.

"March 21." Recent. Dune looked over at Ajana and the girl looked so tired for a teenager, Dune wanted to send her for a nap. The projector offered up more aerial views of Detroit at night, most of the lights out except for the odd neon signs that persisted. Then a sketch appeared, looking up at two men standing on a bridge. The angle made it hard to see more than pant legs stretching down from winter coats, hands in pockets. One man was holding a phone in his gloved hand, taking pictures. "Footage from a dandelion growing in cracks on Ambassador Bridge."

The man with the phone spoke first. "You telling me you can't find one single person?"

"There might be a couple. But not really, not really alive, boss. The city got some, the Guard got some. We had militia help pick up everyone we saw after that—fools weren't scared of 'the Black virus,' we called it evacuation. They're gone."

"What a goddamn mess. How the fuck do I sell this?" Snapping shots, photo after photo.

"You kidding me? An empty city where only pure white people can live? This shit will sell itself. You just build the houses. We got comms covered."

"You're a monster."

"But you'll move in, right boss?" The man guffawed.

The recordings finished and there was a dramatic hush in the room. Then Dawud started laughing.

"What?" Ajana looked startled.

Dawud was laughing too hard to share for a second, and Dune thought he might be the first of the next mutation of the disease, laughing to death. The laugh shifted inside itself, though, and then he was bent over, face covered, crying hard. Dune wrapped herself around him, feeling his brother body, his wailing body. She let his pain open her and her tears flowed with his. Ajana reached forward and awkwardly touched Dune's knee, and Dune grabbed the girl's hand, accepting the comfort.

Finally Dawud caught his breath, wiped his face. "It was a land grab? And they fucked it up? Fucking oops, genocide? And they're worried about the fucking message?" He shook his head slowly.

Dune thought that this was bigger than she could manage, it needed some authority. And in the corrupt landscape of American politics, she could think of no appropriate authority. "How do we stop them?"

"We don't know yet where it originated, who these men are. Or who all knows about this. Or how exactly it was disseminated. And there's no way we can show this as our proof." Ajana's hands were so young, holding the cube. Dune thought she was so brave. "But we don't trust whatever their form of justice might be. I'm making this project to teach the babies, so they know when we fight, why we fight."

Dune felt wrung out and clarified. She asked, "How can we help?"

Dune felt Ajana measuring them with her eyes. "Our victory is to deny them the city, to keep Detroit for those who love it."

Dune felt herself hooked again, pulled forward. This, then, was the next step.

chapter twenty-one

With Intention

Dune was in the basement, naked, smeared in blood and dirt. She danced around the city of Detroit on its card tables, undulating towards it in a way her body didn't know to do in its waking life. She was saying things, words, the words of the grievers flowing through her mouth. As she moved around the room she knew it was an incantation, the words began to take shape as they left her mouth, forming themselves in smoke to float across the city—"child, spring, sunset, Mahershalalhashbaz, lush, diaphanous garden, Belle Isle," crowding over the city. And as she danced and watched, the words clustered into a cloud that covered the city. And it began to rain. And where the raindrops fell, green burst forth on the table, on the city, grass, bushes, moss, vine—Detroit became a total wilderness. When Dune was finished, the entire basement was overgrown, including herself. She began laughing, harder and harder until she curled over in laughter. Fetal, she floated, in bliss. She became a full moon over the new city.

Dune came out of the dream flooded in the light of the full moon. She shook Dawud at the shoulders to wake him. He jolted up as usual. Dune felt brief guilt and then calmed him with her hands and her voice, "Sorry. Sorry. I need your help."

"I got jokes right now, but I think they'd be lost on you." Dawud wiped at his eyes, his voice gravel and grump.

Dune was out of the bed, pulling on sweatpants from the floor, a tank top. Dawud scratched his head and kicked off the sheet.

In the kitchen she opened a low cabinet and pulled out the two largest silver mixing bowls she had. She handed one to Dawud and tucked the other under her arm. Then she flew out the back door, into the moonlit yard, the reflected sunlight delineating each branch, dark against dark.

Dawud was moving slower than Dune, but his curiosity was piqued. Dune was already at the pyre, bent down when he stepped outside. She brushed away the top layer of wintry debris in the fire pit, and then scooped up handfuls of ash. Dawud squatted next to her, shaking his head.

"Yo, you really on some hoodoo shit right now. This how we got Captain as our neighbor?"

Dune cocked her head a bit, not meeting his eyes. "No, that was different. This one is more like how we got the growth on Southfield and 8 Mile. For that I used my mother's bones. These ashes belonged to Bethany and to my grandmother, Vivian."

Dawud looked at Dune for a long time as she filled her bowl. With an exhale, he plunged his fingers down into the ashes and closed his eyes. Softer than dirt. His sister had been harder than rock and now she was softer than dirt, mingled with a grand-mother-stranger. He realized he could protest, stake some claim on this last pound of sister. Instead, with reverence, he began to fill up his bowl.

Dune and Dawud helped each other back inside, taking turns

with the door. Their hands felt heavy with more than ash. Dune set her bowl down outside the basement door, pulled the key from between her breasts and opened it. She lifted her bowl and moved confidently down into the dark.

Dawud muttered, descending behind her, "Bats and shit are both part of your crazy, Little Spoon."

In the basement Dune flipped the light on with her elbow and paused for a moment while Dawud took in what was happening. He hadn't seen it since finding Bethany's face, her voice, down here. It was a wilderness, sheets of vines spilling off the table, hanging down from the ceiling, covering the floor. Dune moved comfortably through it all, to Detroit.

The outer rim of the model was growing up and off the table. Dune dropped down, balancing her ashes. Under the table, the vases were shattered pieces held tightly around a massive mound of green and ash.

"Look," she pointed with her chin—the floor of the basement was cracked open and some of the green disappeared into the earth below the table.

She looked back to Dawud then to see if he was ok, if he would be able to help her. He looked so tender and she could see fear fighting with fascination on his face. He hooked his eyes on her and she extended her calm to him. He was careful as he stepped through the vines on the ground and she understood that he knew the truth, the undeniable truth of her magic—that everything was alive here.

She propped her bowl of ashes against her hip and used her heart hand to push vines off of a chair against the wall, setting her bowl down. She took Dawud's elbow and walked him around to the river.

Which, they noticed at the same moment, was no longer a scarf, but now a continuous river. Dune giggled with some delight, watching the water flow the length of the city, crash down the table in a waterfall, loop back under the table through the foliage, and then flow all the way back up to the city's edge. The table's edge.

Dawud touched the water, tasted it, and looked at Dune as if realizing her divinity in that instant.

Dune offered no resistance to the magic, just listened for the next move. When the impulse came, she reached two hands into the bowl Dawud was holding and lifted up ashes. She held them over the water, closing her eyes.

"Dad, Mom. Bethany, Babs. Vivian, Kama. Elouise, Big Lou." Dune saw the faces pass in front of her. She wasn't sure what to say, could just feel within her body the need to beckon spirit, harness god. "Ancestors. Come into the room with us. Whatever you are doing, we ask you to hold this city, to protect us, to give us more time. We will live. We want to live. We need your help. We accept your protection."

With that, she spilled the ash along the river, cutting off the Ambassador Bridge on the Canada side, following the line of bones. She took two more hands of ash and continued spilling the line as far as she could reach, crossing the highways, cutting off Woodward at 8 Mile. She completed the circle with the last of Dawud's ashes and then took his bowl and set it down, picking up the one she had carried down. She held it, offering it to him.

Dawud looked at her, struggling to take in the basement, the magic, and her part in it. Dune said nothing, her eyes non-negotiable.

He took two hands of ashes and turned to face the city. Dune watched his face soften and then split with tears. She knew that impossible feeling of holding the ash of a loved one; she was deeply moved by Dawud holding his sister, holding her grandmother.

Dune stepped closer to him, so his body could feel her nearby. She felt him settle into himself.

"We need magic. We need miracles. We need mystery." With that, Dawud spilled the ashes along the same lines Dune had set, carefully following her lead, her lines, encircling the city.

Dune walked over to the computer and pushed apart the growth until she found the printer. She pulled out the last two pages she'd printed. They were covered, in small print, in the collection of gathered words. She handed a sheet to Dawud, and at the same time they began reading the words. These words—familiar, mundane, sacred—imbued with miracles because they meant so much to the people who spoke them. Imbued with the last life energy of Detroit.

They read in a monotone at first, but then Dawud began to rock and reached over for Dune's hand. She was reading the words when she felt Dawud's magic crackle into her and she went off the page, weaving with and through him like a DNA strand. "Nightshade oxtail clowning twerking/kiss me Charlotte hummingbird/ secret swimming hole/cartwheels Kimmy sister laughing too hard spitting at dinner/Myrtle comfrey newborn/he's having babies!/ whale spotted phosphorescence/earth from space/bamboo temple bell silence prayer/holding hands by the lighthouse/Papa lifting me onto the horse/she tickled me/there's a line where the sky meets/the fetish the ropes the blindfolds flogging the trust the solitude/downward facing chanterelle edible light trails shooting stars/holding the child/running running painting singing/stepping into the ocean, surrendering to the wave/giving it beauty/

letting go letting god letting faith be an act/the sand underfoot the stars up above/the love the love the love the love!"

They stood next to each other, holding on to each other's hands so tightly, quaking, pulsing with spirit. Time passed such that the celestial beings had all moved before they did. After they returned to the separate entities of themselves, Dawud turned to Dune, rubbing ash along her cheeks as he pulled her close and kissed her, rested his forehead against hers, weary and grateful.

They climbed the steps of the basement, bodies bone-tired. The kitchen was awash in the light of the full moon. They were both exhausted, but something wasn't complete.

Dawud stepped up to Dune with no laughter, leaning his body against hers until she was pressed back against the basement door. He was inhaling at her neck, his hands big, grasping her flesh up against him. She slid her sweatpants down around her ankles and propped her foot against the opposite wall, needing this.

He moved his fingers over her, then into her, while she jacked him off slowly, picking up speed with his breath. They didn't speak, just listened to the splash and breath and friction sounds they were making. When they were both ready, with ash and moonlight all over their bodies, they had a different kind of sex; quiet, primal, keening, quick. For the first time, it was the same exact moment when they reached orgasm.

They leaned against the basement door, dripping, gathering breath. Dawud slipped down a bit and picked Dune up over his shoulder, her sweatpants still bunched around her legs. She was too tired to protest, she just laughed, spent, as he carried her upstairs and they collapsed across the bed.

They left a smear on the door, a puddle on the floor. A river, an ocean. Enough.

chapter twenty-two

Getting to Know Murmur City

There was a knocking at the door that startled Dune. When she opened it, cinching her sweatpants tight, Jizo was waiting. He looked up at Dune with wide eyes. Dune was immediately embarrassed—had they left an inappropriate mess downstairs the night before?

"What is it, angelman?" Dawud called from under a pillow. Jizo pounded against the doorframe, and then he ran down the stairs and slowly, lumbering across dimensions, they followed him.

There, at the basement door, was the wilderness.

Dune blinked, shook her head and pinched herself. She was awake. Thick green fern leaves flowed under and over the closed basement door, into and across the hallway, vines hanging down from the ceiling, growing steadily in every direction. They were growing out the back and front doors.

Dune approached the door and saw how the wild shifted at her approach.

"Well. Shit," Dawud whispered behind her.

Dune touched the vines, ran her fingers through them, unafraid. They were of her, they felt familiar, sentient. She put a hand on the door and took a deep breath. When she turned the knob the door sprung open towards her and vines spilled forward. Every inch in front her was dark and verdant, the warmth of the basement now tropical. There was no way through unless she had a machete.

In her heart she knew that she would never cut this growth. The model was no longer for human eyes.

She turned to say something to her boys, to explain herself. Captain had come in and was leaning against the door to the living room. Jizo was holding Dawud's hand, and Dawud was just watching her, free hand at alert.

She turned into the jungle of her basement, placed her hands and face into it. She inhaled the fresh musky scent and felt everyone flow through her, everyone she had witnessed, listened to, burned free over the past months. She saw their faces. They were not as she had last seen them, in death. They were flashing by in their own laughter, their true faces. She felt them all over her body and she was big enough to hold all of them, pouring through her and out into the world.

Buried in the green, she could feel the vines growing wildly throughout the city, across the Ambassador Bridge, across the highways leaving Detroit, around the construction equipment on Grand, under the river water right up to the surface, tangling into boat engines. Dune saw the city, safe from the world with this fecundity.

It was no vision. No science, but no illusion. It was true, and it was done. There would be no more looking back.

The grievers had sacrificed their bodies, but not their love of each other, of Detroit. However this virus was conceived, they had transformed it into a boundary and a tomorrow.

"Thank you," she whispered. "I love you all. We will live."

. . . .

Dune and Dawud rushed to get what they could from the house as the vines spilled out around them and the house started to moan, unmooring. Dune was surprised to find that there wasn't much that felt important to her. Family pictures, the survival packs her parents had created, their love letters, Kama's altar stones and sage bundles, Mama Vivian's radio, Brendon's cameras. She filled a bag with her mother's jewelry and crystals. She grabbed the dirty clothes around her room. All of these things she tossed into the yard. Dawud gathered all of his things in one trip and then helped her grab as many books as they could pull from the library.

In the yard, Captain and Jizo awaited them. Captain was chewing a licorice stick, laughing in disbelief. Dog ran up, barking, pulling at Jizo. The child looked where Dog's nose was pointing and then clapped his hands to his delicate face, pointing down towards the river. Dune dropped the clothes she was holding as her jaw fell open.

Beyond the casinos and the towers of Murmur City, there was now a green wall reaching up to the clouds. A million vines defied gravity, reaching up to create a thick curtain of life, moving in the wind.

It was vast, as Detroit had always been vast. The boundary created a new geography by liberating a known one, protecting a precious Black realm.

The lush border ran the length of the river, as far as she could see in both directions. Turning, she could only see the very top of it far off to the east, far off to the west and the north, opening to the sky. Dune knew the exact lines of these walls; she could still feel each pound of bones and ashes in her hands. Now they were in a bowl of fecundity, a valley for Detroit, of Detroit. The green wall was mountainous, like being at the base of a new canyon. It was the largest structure she had ever seen, the largest magic she could imagine.

After some time, quietly, they loaded everything into the car, unable to take their eyes off the green wall and the house that birthed it. Dune held the porch banister one last time, offering gratitude. Then, Dog running along beside them, they drove to Murmur City.

. . . .

The air was thick with fog for a long time, Dune reached through it with her fingers stretched ahead of her, feeling suffocated by the moisture against her face. She focused, breathing slow enough to find the air in the water. Then she came through to a clear place, the fog holding at the edges like trees holding secrets, like the sea holds an island.

In the clear place there is no one. And then Kama is there, then Mama Vivian, and Elouise, Brendon, Big Lou. They are themselves, but they are also made of the fog. Dune looked at her hands to see if she, too, was made of the fog, but she was just flesh.

Kama called her over with her hand, with a sound, and Dune was next to her mother. Everyone crowded around her then and she felt the whisper of their touches on her forehead, neck, her chin, the soft rolls of her back, her belly, her thighs. She felt held, every inch of her, for a length of dream time.

Then everyone was gone but Kama. Kama began to undo, to be less herself and more fog. Dune reached towards her and Kama crystallized again. Dune could see her face so clearly, could see the love in her eyes.

"Baby." Kama finally spoke to her directly. "Stop feeding us."

chapter twenty-three

Together

Dear Moms and Dad,

Thank you for saving my life. Over and over. Directly and through all the books you left behind, and the model of Detroit. And the ideas you planted all around me—the formations you dreamed and seeded will be the foundation of my life. I was never lost, forgotten, overlooked as you made these plans—y'all left me everything I needed.

Thank you. I am in community now. I'm going to make it.

Love,

Dune

. . . .

"Here. We. Are! And we are the champions, my friends, we are the ones who won at death. We learned to grieve, to grieve most excellently. Grief is gratitude. Without it we are ingrates, we don't get the blessings. But when we grieve most excellently, the sun shines upon us. It isn't stealth we need now, but faith, because someone is coming for our sacred land."

Dawud was in the broadcast room of Murmur City, holding a small microphone with a ringlet of cord. When he spoke he pressed a button on the side of the microphone and, as long as the green light was on, he could easily send his message out to the entire seven building system. They had asked him to do a weekly broadcast and he was pleased to be able to do it. It was the thing that came easiest to him now. The *Everything Awesome Circus* felt different, more grounded and at ease. This was his offering of gratitude for their welcome to this place.

Dune sat next to him, watching him with a little wonder. She was tousled, they had had a good morning together. She had a set of rooms with him in what they called Sea Tower, down the hall from Captain and Jizo. Rio had claimed a lovers' room in Wind Tower to use when Dune was ready.

Rio's apocalypse partner Sahari had come back from a reconnaissance trip to the northern edge of the city. She was vibrant, wonderful, regaling the community with stories of the vine border bursting into existence before her eyes. She lived with Rio in a space they'd shared in the Wildfire Tower for months.

There was peace, there was pleasure, there was plenty. There was the thick wild new border around them, which made them all feel freer, safer.

And there was purpose in their campaign to understand and discourage recolonization by the orange suits. There was a future for all of them, crafted from the work they did in and from this building, reaching and reclaiming this city, reclaiming its fecundity.

They were tracking threats of H-8 spreading and it wasn't clear how to fight on that front. But they'd begun a careful negotiation by radio communications through the National Guard, building a case for sovereignty. They would live and they would fight to do that living here.

"Everyone grab the person close to you, it may be more than one person. It may be a group. But grab it, them, he, she, grab them! And here is what to do. Turn and face them and say this:

"'You are a miracle!' Say it!

"'I love myself!

"'This city is not for sale!' Say it loud, let me hear you!

"'We are the small committed band of rebels that we always fetishized! Let us make today a liberation!'

"Now pour a libation. It can be that most precious resource of water, or it may be something more delicious or nutritious. Take a deep breath. We have only just begun. We are in the birth canal my loves, shit we *are* the birth canal!

"Press on."

Epilogue

Dune was moving down the hallway, two weeks after moving into Murmur City. They had an astounding view of the river up towards Belle Isle and the east side of Detroit.

She was learning how to gather rations and contribute to the production of food, volunteering in the greenhouse. Dawud entertained, Captain entertained and shocked, and Jizo delighted. Dog was with them, and seemed excited by all of the new humans to relate to.

Dune felt a sense of lost time or capacity since leaving her mother's home. She had fulfilled her purpose, perhaps now her mutation was complete. She didn't know if her magic could work without the basement, the model, the altar her parents had left her. She wasn't even quite sure where she was heading, though she'd probably end up in her gardening gloves, attending to the beauty that would become dinner.

In an instant that seemed both supernatural and increasingly familiar, Mama Rue stepped in front of Dune. Did the woman plot these encounters? Stalk her? Before Dune could wonder whether to feel unnerved or special, Mama Rue pinned her into the present moment, her eyes empty of anything soft or slow. Dune felt it was useless to resist Mama Rue, even as the eldest grabbed Dune's wrist hard enough to promise a bruise. "You know. You *know*."

Dune froze, feeling exposed. Did Mama Rue mean her mutation, her power that she did not know how to harness? Dune felt like she knew nothing. The city had responded to her. For months she'd felt her mother's presence when she woke up and, even now, far from her house, she kept getting glimpses of a past, or a future. But for all she felt and saw and did, she wasn't sure she *knew* anything.

"Know what?" She tried to sound innocent, but, vocalized, she sounded foolish and young.

"They are here! They are all here!" Mama Rue whispered, grinning and gorgeous, her eyes wide on Dune, looking into her, through her, inhaling in blameless awe. "They lost all around us and they need us to help 'em get home!"

Dune's thoughts flooded with her loved ones' faces and the glimpses of Detroit from her dreams, her dreams of Kama, her dreams of life beyond these bodies. Her thoughts were naked, that's how it felt, like nothing she was thinking was private, but projected across the space between her and Mama Rue, bright as a projector in a dark room. Could Mama Rue see what Dune had only admitted in her dreams? Were the dreams even hers to claim?

"They are here, Dunechild! They are right here!" Mama Rue laughed in a shout.

"They
did
not
die."

Acknowledgments

Jacob Dorn for the idea of the walking house, generated in a sci-fi youth workshop at the Grace and James Boggs School.

Imani Perry for a reframe on how we write Black and White in our current context, read *South to America*.

Mama Sandra, the Reverend Sandra Simmons, who became an ancestor during the writing of this text. She taught us, "We must live and not die."